ISLANDS AT WAR

ISLANDS AT WAR by Chris Lake:
ISBN 1 870544 05 6

Published by Redberry Press, Trinity, Jersey
Printed by Cox and Wyman Ltd, Reading Berks
Cover: Stewart Redway Associates

With special thanks to Harry Patterson

The characters in this novel and their actions and personalities are imaginary. Their names and experiences have no relation to those of actual people, alive or dead, except by coincidence.

Foreword

'By March 1945 Allied forces had swept across Europe, the end of the war only weeks away. The Channel Islands had been left in German hands rather than run the risk of the heavy civilian casualties which would have resulted from a direct attack. And yet it was at this time that the German authorities decided to mount one of the most audacious commando attacks of the entire war, and from St Helier, in Jersey.

'The target was Granville on the French coast, then occupied by American forces. The attack force consisted of six minesweepers, three torpedo boats, two converted landing craft and several other vessels, and the naval and military personnel involved amounted to some 800 men.

'After hard fighting, Granville was successfully secured, an American torpedo boat was sunk in a naval action and the German forces returned to St Helier with various captured vessels, some 30 prisoners, including several Americans, and 55 German prisoners of war who had been released.

'An episode of war, little known even to most Jersey people, has now been recreated as fiction in 'ISLANDS AT WAR', without doubt one of the finest books to have emerged from the German occupation of Jersey.'

Jack Higgins, June 1992

To my father

1

Who Pays the Ferryman?

Extract from 'Memoirs of an Infantry Officer', by Siegfried Sassoon

The lecturer's voice still battered on my brain: 'The bullet and the bayonet are brother and sister. If you don't kill him, he'll kill you. Stick him between the eyes, in the throat, in the chest. Don't waste good steel. Six inches are enough – what's the use of a foot of steel sticking out at the back of a man's neck? Three inches will do for him; when he coughs, go and look for another.'

'GREYS and blues,' thought Lieutenant Muskie, as he looked out across the sea and then back to the harbour and the sky above. 'Granville is a combination of greys and blues. Blue sea, grey sky. Grey buildings, blue sky. No matter what the time of day or the mood you're in the colours remain the same.'

He shrugged his shoulders and went in. This was Normandy, 10 August, 1944, and he hated the town almost as much as he hated the hotel. He hated the town not because it wasn't pretty – which it was – but because it was French; he much preferred the warmer skies and sunnier beaches of California. He hated the hotel because although large and imposing, with an imperial style far outstripping the other, lesser hotels and guest houses near the harbour, it was much too big and impersonal for such a humble town. It was also past its best, whenever that had been. 'Before the turn of the last century,' Muskie guessed. But he hated the hotel most of all because of the small rooms they had found upstairs – the dormer rooms beneath the eaves.

He had been warned about those rooms by the GIs who had driven out the Germans nearly three weeks ago – ten days before he'd arrived to set up headquarters for his boss, General Dwight D Eisenhower, Supreme Commander of all the Allied forces, as they prepared to move south and west, to St Malo.

It wasn't booby traps he had to worry about that first time as he climbed the five flights of stairs to the upstairs rooms; it was the purpose to which those rooms had been put. Originally staff quarters for the hotel, they were cramped and functional, with square walls and sloping ceilings. But under the Germans, and in particular the Gestapo, who had held the Hotel Normandie for two years as a so-called centre of intelligence, each room had been divided into two: an inner cell, with no windows, and an outer cell with two wooden chairs, a desk and, in some cases, glorious views across the bay. The contrast between those rooms and the rooms in the rest of the hotel made a mockery of all that a seaside holiday hotel ought to be. Three floors down you could spend up to 80 francs a night for a balcony room, thick pile carpet, velvet curtains and a four-poster bed, but here, in these cramped attic rooms, you paid for your bed and board with pain and blood.

It was the inner room which was the real obscenity; especially if you had a good imagination or had ever seen the Gestapo at work. For although there was a connecting door between the cells, there was only one handle and lock to each door, and both were on the outside.

And inside?

When the liberators arrived there had been no prisoners to rescue. God alone knows where they were now. But inside the bleak, bare white rooms there had been hooks – the kind of hook you would see hammered into a butcher's shop wall, with carcasses of meat hanging up ready to be trimmed and sold. Beneath the hooks in every room had been stains. Dried bloodstains on the scrubbed wooden floor.

'Interrogation can mean many things to many people,' thought Muskie as he pushed open the wide double doors leading into the hotel and headed towards the main reception area. But the icy stillness of those rooms lingered in his mind. It was a stillness which reminded him of when he was a kid playing hide and seek with his brothers. You sensed when you walked into a room that someone was there, holding his breath, not wanting to be found. If they'd hidden themselves well, you wouldn't find them – but they were there, you knew that. Here, however, in those bare cells there was nowhere to hide and no-one to see. But the hair still bristled at the back of your neck and you would swear that if you listened hard enough you could hear someone breathing. Dead breath in a haunted room: Lieutenant Muskie shivered at the memory of that uncomfortable silence, and the bloodstains which served as a reminder that interrogation, to the Gestapo, could be a terribly messy business.

'Still,' he thought, 'this is war and the good guys do seem to be coming out on top.'

Muskie eased his way past the soldier on reception, who acknowledged his appearance in the hotel with a brief nod, before turning left, to where the ballroom had been, now the nerve centre of SHAEF, Supreme Headquarters, Allied Expeditionary Forces, whose aim was to rid western France of all pockets of German resistance as soon as possible.

At the back of the room secretaries were busy typing; in another part men and women in uniform or civilian clothes were either busily engaged on the phone or reading their way through what appeared to be mountains of paper. Muskie took in all that was happening at a glance, reflecting that it was this administration of war which appealed to him the least, before turning towards three men, two in uniform and one in polo-neck jumper and corduroy trousers, who were looking at a collection of maps pinned to the wall near one of the large bay windows.

They were too deep in conversation to bother much with his approach at first, until the oldest of the three, a bull-necked officer of medium height, high forehead and clear blue eyes said: 'Hi, Mike, good to see you. Nice to have you back with us.'

'Just taking in the sights, General,' said Muskie, as his commanding officer shook his hand firmly, before introducing him to the others.

'Mike Muskie,' the General said, 'meet Major Harding of the British Special Air Service force and George Leighton, who's been working for us for the last few weeks behind enemy lines. You might have heard of George: without him we'd probably still be on Utah beach building sandcastles. George Leighton, Major Harding, meet Mike Muskie. He's been posted here for the next few months, although I know he's dying to get back into the thick of things again. Seems some men can't get enough of war – isn't that right, George?'

Eisenhower gave a wry smile as he looked at the slightly-built man standing next to him. You wouldn't look twice at him in a crowd; he was neither scruffy nor smart, had sparse dark brown hair combed forward, in the French style, and seemed almost apologetic to be in such illustrious company. But neither Ike Eisenhower nor Muskie were fooled; they both knew about this man who, with the code-name François, had helped the French resistance movement to delay by almost two weeks the entire 2nd SS Panzer Division from reaching Normandy from Toulouse.

The journey should have taken three days, but by assiduously blowing up every German petrol dump along the way and by continual acts of sabotage, François and his men had forced the division to abandon the road and travel instead by rail. Then it had been the turn of another British agent, Louis Philippe de Cuirot – codenamed Cyrano – and those under his command to take control. By blowing up the railway bridges between Bergerac and Périgueux they had forced the division further east, where another Special Operations Executive circuit, led by Jacques Briault – Blanco – set up a series of ambushes around

Brive and Tulle. Not until 18 June had the division reached its reserve positions near Torigni, Canisy and Tess – seventeen days after they had been ordered north and twelve days too late to help drive the Allies back to the beach.

The introductions continued.

'Before the war Major Harding had a holiday cottage not far away at Portbail. Seems he spent every summer he could on vacation there,' the General said.

Muskie knew little about this second man, although his uniform told him he was British, and the fact that he was a major suggested he was a regular soldier, a career man, and not a conscript who had joined the war by default rather than design.

'Major Harding will be leaving in a couple of days for Rennes,' Eisenhower continued. 'Once he gets there he's a little business to attend to behind enemy lines.'

Lieutenant Muskie saluted. It was an instinctive thing to do, not least because he respected brave men and knew that this kind of 'little business' must, inevitably, jeopardise the Major's life. Any Allied soldiers found behind German lines were currently being shot, out-of-hand, by the enemy. As they found themselves pulling further and further back to the east they no longer respected the niceties of war – there'd been enough reports of how brutally they had behaved to confirm that – and, unless he was an exceptional man, within a couple of weeks Roy Harding could easily become just another corpse shot and dumped unceremoniously into a roadside ditch. Not that the prospect seemed to worry the Major. He was about 5 ft 10 ins tall, lean and craggy, so beanpole-thin that if he bent double you could imagine him snapping; but his military bearing was all you'd expect of an English officer, with the one difference that he seemed more relaxed, sardonic even, than most other serving officers.

'Pleased to meet you,' the Major said, not in the clipped tones that Muskie expected but with the warm burr of a Dorset accent, unfamiliar to the American.

The other man – George Leighton – hadn't as yet said anything. Seemingly more intent on chain-smoking some foul-smelling French cigarettes than conversation, he gave a brief nod to Muskie as Eisenhower turned to a larger map pinned to the wall to run a finger down the coast from Cherbourg to a small town in Brittany.

'St Malo will have to fall soon,' he said, tapping the map with his forefinger. 'They can't hold out for much longer.'

'The sea's their lifeline at the moment, sir,' said Harding. 'That's where the help's coming from.'

The Major reached out and touched the map further up the coast, nearer to Granville than St Malo, where four small islands were scattered together in a clump about twenty miles due west of the Cotentin peninsula. 'The Channel Islands. Occupied by Jerry for the past four years. What Hitler calls "The Fortress Islands" – every one of them reinforced and heavily armed, waiting for a British counter-attack that never came. Over the past few years they've poured enough concrete into them to sink a dozen smaller islands. They're very very pretty in spring, but for the past four years have been occupied by German troops with nothing much to do and nowhere to run. But we daren't attack them for fear of reprisals.'

There was a pause as the Major waited for the General to comment, but it was Leighton who spoke next, talking quickly, in a low, dispassionate voice which the others had to strain their ears to hear. It was a rasping voice, which bore testimony to the many cigarettes he had chain-smoked his way through during the four years of the war. Anticipating Eisenhower's half-asked question, he said: 'They're ours, you see, British.

'We sort of abandoned them at the start of the war and there must be – oh, I suppose 50,000 or so British citizens living there, under German control.'

He paused, choosing his words carefully. 'Of course if the Germans there ever *did* decide to leave the islands, if they tried to make a fight of it instead of pussy-footing their way through the war, we'd have problems.

'Until recently, when they began to send supplies by sea to

St Malo, taking out wounded soldiers by return, they showed no interest whatsoever in becoming involved in the fighting – and even then it was only token support to their beleaguered garrison. And yet there must be as many as 25,000 fighting men on Jersey and Guernsey alone – more with the other islands – so if they did decide to make a go of it, well I for one wouldn't like to be the one to get in their way.'

There was a matter-of-fact tone to Leighton's voice, as if he were well used to getting in the way of angry Germans, and although Muskie never met the man again after he and Harding set off for Rennes four days later, he couldn't shake off Leighton's words or his calm indifference, his shrug-of-the-shoulders approach to war, as if it were merely there to be getting along with until something more important came along.

It was only later, when he compared the mood of the two men he'd seen that day, that Muskie realised that while Major Harding saw war with the detached eye of the professional – as the justification for choosing the army as his career – to Leighton it meant something very different. He remembered the conversation he'd had with him later that night, a conversation which showed Leighton to be a warm, humorous man, soft-spoken and self-effacing. But in his pale blue eyes and conversation was an emptiness which was very different from his own thirst for life.

Somehow their conversation had turned to religion, and on whose side God might be in this terrible war. To Leighton God's role was irrelevant; but so, too, were compassion, love, friendship and, by the same token, hate, anger and revenge. 'Everything,' he said, 'was of equal value.' The past four years had taught him this.

He had, he said, no illusions any more; no illusions about how cruel man could be, and no illusions about the meaning of life in general and his own in particular. 'Everything is of equal importance,' he said in that quick, throaty voice. 'A flea or a man. They are of equal value and by the same token if you seek for God in one, you must seek for God in the other. Everything. Nothing. Two words with the same meaning. But we carry on, living the lie. . .' He smiled, as if to reassure the tall American that this was only his own, personal philosophy, a legacy of having had the mystique of death and the sanctity of life torn away from him not once, but many times during his encounters with Germans.

Muskie, however, wasn't entirely convinced that Leighton had denied all human emotion to the extent that life and death had the same value – or rather lack of it – as swollen feet or toothache. 'He's a man looking for something to believe in,' Muskie decided. 'He's looking for a way to save his soul.'

But if war had scarred Leighton so badly, for Muskie, who had joined the war less than sixth months before, it had been an interesting conversation with no real substance. He could pity Leighton, pity him for slipping so far down into the black hole of despair, but he couldn't agree with his bleak outlook, his almost nihilist self-analysis which ultimately led nowhere. Muskie wasn't going nowhere; far from it. And just as he had already enjoyed a brief engagement with the enemy, so he had too much fight left in him not to want more. He'd not come all this way to become a filing clerk. The moments of adventure he'd had so far he'd thoroughly enjoyed. He was a fighter, enjoying both the hunt and the kill, and there was enough war remaining, he reckoned, even at this late hour, to get a great deal more of both.

2

Sleepless nights

NO lights, no introduction, just the gentle opening of the door and fumbling hands beneath the bedspread, General-leutnant von Schellenberg remembered, as he cupped the young girl's breast in his hand and pulled her gently towards him in the big double bed.

He had not wanted her; indeed, when General-major Kaarlson had brought the two girls round that evening, joking with them and flirting outrageously, knowing how impressed they would be to be invited to the Kommandant's house, he had refused to join in with their coarse and lusty conversation. He had not wanted either girl, and had slipped away at midnight, complaining of too much work to do the next day, leaving them to their games and laughter. True, both girls had been very pretty – and available – but he was in no mood for such temporary pleasures of the flesh. And when, half-drowsy and thinking of tomorrow, he had felt that first soft and very unsubtle hand caress his thigh, he had pulled away, wanting no more than to be left alone. It had been she, like a seasoned professional, who had urged herself forward, and although it wasn't love and didn't pretend to be, the touch and warmth of the young girl's flesh, her ability to mould herself to his body and his need for something other than the hollowness of his military life had prompted him to demand her, to take what was offered in frantic, urgent sexual release. It was, after all, good sex with no half-hearted pretence of good love, and his body had enjoyed every minute of it.

Besides, he told himself afterwards, the bed was too big for one, and he mentally thanked the good Major Kaarlson for showing such concern for his sexual appetite, although it had been later, much later, as she lay fleshily asleep in his arms that he appreciated her most. The intimacy of touch and the warmth of her young body was far more reassuring than any temporary sexual release on crimson sheets in a foreign island so far from home.

It wasn't the first time that von Schellenberg had succumbed to casual sex but he had long been disappointed by the direct approach of the English girls, preferring instead the coquettish flirtation of the French. He knew that with the English girls that it was going to bed with the Island Kommandant or Befehlshaber which excited them most. He was under no illusions about his looks; though fit for his age, without an excess ounce of fat on his lean frame, he was well aware that he was old enough to be the father of some of the girls he'd taken. The consolation was that unlike an inexperienced youth of 18, he didn't demand anything and everything a girl's body could provide, and thought a good deal about the girl's enjoyment as well as his own. He could play the game well, occasionally making believe that sex, for its own sake, had some finer value, and that it made no difference to the very real love he had for his wife back home in Germany.

He moved his left hand down gently, towards the soft curve of the girl's belly and pulled her closer, playing spoons with her naked body in his, thinking of home with a vague feeling of guilt as he remembered the last letter he had received from his wife – a letter not from their Schloss high in the hills in Bavaria, but a letter smuggled out from somewhere in Lotz, where she had been taken for interview six days before. He knew she was alive; he knew that she was innocent of taking any part in the Valkyrie plot against the Führer; he also knew that sooner or later he, too, would have to answer some very difficult questions. For now, however, he could take comfort in this young girl's ripening body, so warm and so soft.

'Tomorrow – tomorrow we shall play at being at war again,' he promised himself lazily, before falling into a deep but troubled sleep.

3

A very long memory

'DO not,' said Vice-admiral Kreiser, 'do not forget, Herr Kommandant, that I have a very long memory. . .'

'How could I forget, Admiral Kreiser?' von Schellenberg replied, with the air of someone who had heard the same thing over and over again and was bored by the repetition. 'But no, I will not prosecute more people than I have to. This war, Herr Admiral, is more important than the petty crimes of a few islanders stupid enough to listen to the BBC on their hidden radios and even more stupid to get caught.

'And no, I will not imprison islanders without good reason. The jail is already over-full and there is a waiting list of other law-breakers ordered to be thrown inside. So I will not prosecute this Mr Drew. There will be no prosecution. It will serve no purpose.'

'Very well,' said Kreiser, 'but you will regret this. Sooner or later your apparent reluctance to administer the law efficiently will be known in Berlin, and the Führer will realise that you are already thinking about defeat. Such knowledge, I believe, will come sooner to Herr Hitler than later. Good day to you.'

Vice-Admiral Kreiser clicked his heels in salute, gave a brief, discourteous bow and left the room.

As the door closed behind the pompous little seaman, the Kommandant smiled a smile of resignation which contained no warmth. It was the smile of a man with too many preoccupations and little comfort in the future, although his eyes lost that weary look when the girl on reception phoned to tell him that Hoffmeister was on his way up to see him. This was good news.

The 'come in' was barely necessary, for by the time he'd finished the sentence, the large, confident man, mid-way between youth and middle age was at his desk. A languid Hitler salute and warm handshake were followed by genuine warmth and affection as both men relaxed in each other's company. They never lied to each other, accepted each other's strengths and weaknesses and had the same pragmatic view of the war. It would be a good war to win, a dreadful war to lose, especially if their leaders went down demanding that their army fight tooth and nail to the finish, exacting terrible revenge on their enemy as they slithered to defeat.

Wilhelm Hoffmeister had an American look to him: square-jawed, with blond hair curt short, and a hard, thin mouth beneath eyes surrounded by thin lines etched finely into his skin. His eyes were pale blue, intelligent and piercing; eyes which looked directly into yours when he spoke. His build, and the crooked nose, bent and broken many years ago in a street fight, gave him the appearance of a boxer, a sport he'd enjoyed in pre-war days when he'd fought at light-middleweight for the army. Bulkier now – middleweight going on heavyweight – he was an excellent soldier who was entering the best period of his soldiering career. No longer hot-headed or foolhardy, he had the advantage of age on his side; age and the learnt ability to consider events very carefully before wading into action. He was content with life, knew the world well enough, and years before had decided that life had no spiritual meaning; you took what you could, laughed when you could, and tried to extract every ounce of pleasure from it without having to pay over the odds for such amusement.

He contrasted markedly with von Schellenberg, the German autocrat, straight-backed, well aware of his height, which he used to good effect to dominate such people such as Kreiser, and used to hiding his true feelings in the Prussian tradition. If he had been a harder man he could have used his position to rule by intimidation, but there was an innate sense of fair play to all men which prevented this, a quality much appreciated by his friends, but a quality seen as a weakness by the likes of the fussy Vice-Admiral.

Von Schellenberg was a good man and an intelligent leader, and men respected his authority, not least because he would listen to them and would not allow himself to condemn out of hand. Equally, the majority of the islanders, who would never have admitted to liking a German, respected him and, if pressed, would agree that he showed genuine concern for most of their problems.

Hoffmeister was more of an unknown quantity to the island community, although the soldiers he commanded spoke highly of him. He never spoke down (or up) to anyone and, if he couldn't do the job himself, wouldn't complain about others not doing it for him. Unlike other regular soldiers in the island, he didn't wile away the hours complaining about the raw, lily-livered type of soldier the Führer was sending them these days. Colonel Hoffmeister was also very much a fighting man, broad and leathery, with a creased face etched with lines around the mouth and eyes. He had a penchant for telling the truth, when it needed to be told, no matter how much it might get him into trouble. His friendship with von Schellenberg hadn't been without incident in the past, and on more than one occasion the Kommandant had had to argue his friend's corner, or else see him perish – victim of some incautious remark made to the wrong sort of people. Beneath it all, however, he was loyal first to his friends, secondly to his country and thirdly to the Führer. He was a soldier by choice, and had climbed through the ranks after serving with the infantry in the First World War. He had known General von Schellenberg since the 1920s.

It had been Hoffmeister who, only a month ago, had found Dr Hucknall's cellar full of more food than one man could eat in a year at a time when the rest of the island had been reduced to eating dandelion soup or limpets taken from the rocks at low tide. And it had been von Schellenberg who, at Hoffmeister's suggestion, had put on show the contents of Dr Hucknall's cellar in a shop window in the heart of the island capital, St Helier – a move which had turned the islanders against the doctor, who was subsequently vilified and shunned like a leper. Von Schellenberg, Hoffmeister knew, had been tempted to throw Hucknall to the mercy of his own people but had decided against it, knowing they would have strung him up for keeping such a hoard of food to himself when they were starving. So he had ordered him to be locked into the already overcrowded cells for his own protection where, even in jail, he had become suddenly accident prone. His fellow Jersey prisoners took advantage, whenever their guards weren't looking, to make their feelings known. They didn't like hoarders, profiteers and Germans, and as Hucknall fitted easily into the first two categories he was fair game for a poke in the eye or an elbow dug deeply into his over-full belly.

'The others will be here soon, Herr Kommandant,' said Hoffmeister. 'I did as you ordered. Four of them – although I still think you were wrong to ignore young Lindau. He, more than any other soldier, is itching for action and will want to know why you haven't considered him.'

'No. Four men are all we need at this stage,' said von Schellenberg. If we need him later we can draft him in.'

He could have added: 'And I want him to stay out of harm's way, because he is my wife's nephew,' but he didn't, and instead walked over to another table at the back of the room. This was covered by a large white tablecloth, which he pulled away. Beneath it was what appeared to be a children's toy – a rough, toytown village complete with small houses and shops, all carefully labelled, including a toytown harbour with ships and jetties and, on the cliffs to the west of the old town, a radar station and bunker.

'Granville,' said von Schellenberg. 'Exact to the smallest detail, as we were promised. At one time host to 193 Division, before they were forced to travel south. Now headquarters for the Allied Command, and the allied commander, the American, General Eisenhower.

'I hope you have acquainted yourself with this general,' said von Schellenberg, suddenly animated. 'General Dwight D Eisenhower, who will be made very welcome when he makes an unexpected visit to our island fortress in three weeks' time.'

* * * *

WHEN they assembled, General von Schellenberg looked around and wished that he, too, was 20 years younger. Forty-six wasn't a great age, but for the work he had in store for them you needed the optimism of youth and a blind belief that no-one could kill you. He no longer shared that belief.

'Gentlemen . . .' he said as he looked around, 'Gentlemen, before I outline your part in the raid planned for the French sea-side port of Granville. . .'

There was a sudden alertness, as he knew there would be, at the prospect of action against the enemy in France.

'Before I explain your part in the raid I will repeat to you a story, a true tale that some of you may have already heard as rumour, although this, and much else that I will tell you, must remain secret from even the men you command.'

By the look on the faces he could see that each, in his own way, was intrigued, and perhaps, he hoped, a little proud that of all the men under his command he had chosen them to share this secret with – whatever it might be.

What they would not realise, thought von Schellenberg to himself as he looked at each in turn, waiting for the full effect of what he had said to sink in, was that by implication what he had said and what he was about to say could ruin his career for ever. In his face and in his words they must see only strength; they must also use their imaginations to look ahead, to what might happen if the Anglo-American forces continued to drive them back, deep into Germany, back towards Hitler and Berlin. He also had to convince them that the raid would succeed, for if there were doubts, and if these were expressed strongly enough to Kreiser, there was still time for a rapid recall to Berlin. And Berlin was the last place he wanted to be.

He looked at the men again. He had trusted Hoffmeister to find them, and now he had to trust his good friend's judgement of character. As he continued to speak he was putting names to faces, remembering some of the details about each man. Hoffmeister had compiled the report. Less formal and more direct than their official listings, it was now tucked away in his drawer.

Jacob Kesselring was the oldest of the party. His brother had been one of the last recruits in the First World War. Within a few days of being sent to the trenches, he had died there. On the surface Kesselring seemed to have no trace of bitterness about his brother's death, nor that of his mother, who had died of grief six months later. Kesselring was courteous to the islanders, quiet, bookish even, but on the battlefield he pursued the enemy with no thoughts of his own safety. He killed ruthlessly and efficiently, and for five months on the Russian Front butchered men with fierce intensity. He did so with a bayonet; bullets being too precious in the wasteland of Russia, where he had mastered the art of lunging, twisting and pulling the blade out of the wound to perfection, although at first he had relied too much on his own brute strength. Push the blade in too hard and it could snag, becoming impossible to remove without the added and wasteful complication of a bullet to enlarge the hole. Three inches into the head or heart ensured a kill; more than that and you were wasting effort and time. The secret was to aim impassionately and accurately, and not to flinch as the blade crunched bone.

Nicolas Jagmann: mad about motorbikes, women and his own physique; a man to whom other men naturally gravitated. Very much the survivor. Not, perhaps, a born leader like Hoffmeister, whose own instinct for survival was coupled with a desire that his men, too, should survive with him, Jagmann could never be accused of being a cautious man. But then his casual approach denied the fact that if he said it would be done, he would do it. How well Jagmann could keep a secret von Schellenberg didn't know, but if he could keep details of the raid as secret as the number and quality of women he had enjoyed he would be well satisfied. It was said that women were especially grateful to Jagmann because afterwards he would never boast about his conquests. Afterwards, and during these affairs, their husbands would never know of his cuckolding ways.

Franz Lindenheim: the perfectionist; always immaculately groomed, even to the extent of having brought two monogrammed dressing gowns with him to the island. He could have been any age, with that closely trimmed pointed beard and hair swept back high from his forehead, but the file showed he was only 34. He was uncomplicated, lacking in imagination perhaps, but the most reliable of the four because he lived his life by the rule book. Before the war he had been captain of a whaling ship; now he was to be entrusted with leading a small German fleet to Granville and bringing it back again intact, accompanied by as many prize vessels as possible from the small French harbour.

Von Schellenberg knew a little of the history of these off-island waters, and knew that in the 17th century Jersey, Alderney and Guernsey privateers had grown rich by plucking prize vessels and their cargoes from the sea and holding them to ransom. History would now repeat itself; but it would be the German navy who would do the stealing, not a cut-throat band of Channel Island privateers.

Finally von Schellenberg's eyes fixed on Otto von Bastion, the baby of the group, and he knew there was a fanaticism in the way he had devoted himself so completely to the Führer's vast ambition which was almost inhuman. Only when he spoke of his beloved leader did he become in any way animated, and there was something decidedly odd about the young man, with the receding, sandy hair, high forehead and bright blue eyes, bulging out from the sallowness of his face. Two years in the island and very much the unknown quantity of the group, he was twenty-one years old and a product of the Hitler Youth movement. After several years of learning how to destroy life and property, he wanted nothing more than to do just that. Hoffmeister said von Bastion admired the Kommandant and could be trusted because of that admiration and because of his desire to put his skills to good use. Von Schellenberg hoped, for all their sakes, that the Colonel's faith in the youngster was justified.

Two army lieutenants, one Oberleutnant, one lieutenant-colonel or Oberstleutnant and one naval Kapitan zur See who, between them, would lead this raid on France. Although von Schellenberg enjoyed the power of command that his uniform and position gave him, he needed these men first as friends, second as subordinates if the raid was to go ahead as planned.

He continued: 'Two weeks ago Horst Ziegler and five others from 219 Company, prisoners of the Americans and assigned to work on the harbour at Granville, unloading coal, escaped from captivity.

'They did this by breaking through a small window in their cell. Then, under the cover of darkness just after midnight and having stolen a tender to one of the cargo ships, they rowed towards the islands.

'If they had been seen they would have been shot, but it wasn't until they approached the Minquiers, a group of rocks midway between France and Jersey, that they were challenged.

'Only the bad shooting of our own marines, stationed on the rocky outcrop, saved their lives. Der Marineartillerie thought they were being attacked by a small British or American raiding party and opened fire, damn near killing them all. It was only when Ziegler swore loudly at them in German that they had sense enough to stop. Anything else and we might never have seen them again.

'It took them another five hours to row to the island, against the tide, but they made the crossing without further mishap and were greeted as heroes when they told us what they had done. After a good night's sleep they were debriefed, here, at my headquarters, and under orders from Berlin were sent on the next plane home. Only Ziegler stayed behind; he'd been hit in the leg by a bullet when the marines opened fire, and needed hospital treatment.

'That bullet wound saved Ziegler's life. The plane the other four were on was intercepted and destroyed over Germany two hours after it took off. There were no survivors.'

There was a silence as each man in the room remembered the four young men who had preferred to make a break for home instead of living out the rest of the war under British and American command.

'Already what I am telling you is new. Only a few of us on the island know of the deaths of these men. The decision not to tell the troops was a deliberate one. To reveal that all five would be alive today if they had remained in enemy hands would undermine morale, already at a low ebb, still further. So much wasted heroism, blown out of the sky. . . which is also the reason Ziegler was sent home as quickly as possible after being discharged from hospital. If he had stayed he would have wanted to know what had happened to his friends; and if he had known, the rest of the island would soon have known too.'

There was a nervous shifting in seats, but no-one spoke, although von Schellenberg noticed that von Bastion was looking at him with a half-puzzled look, as if to say he hadn't volunteered his services to listen to this. The deaths of these four men meant nothing to him; he had been promised action, not apologies and recrimination.

Von Schellenberg became more positive, gaining strength, perhaps, from their silence.

'Those men's lives, gentlemen, will not be wasted. We will not allow them to be wasted.'

He moved away from the desk and walked towards the model on the table, which he and Hoffmeister had brought forward to the middle of the room.

'This, gentlemen,' he said, 'this is a model – an accurate model in every detail – of the town of Granville as it is today. It was built with the help of Ziegler and his men, who described in fine detail the layout of the town, where French, British and American soldiers have been quartered and where General Eisenhower has made his base.

'Take a good look at it. The better you know the town, the more that knowledge will help to save your lives.'

The four officers did so, realising that they weren't looking at it to admire the skill of the model-maker but to learn street names, to evaluate distances, to get to know this foreign town as if they had lived there since birth.

'A typical small French holiday town, by the look of it,' said Lindenheim, although it has an unusual number of cargo vessels in the harbour.'

'Yes, but where are the girls on the beach for Nikki?' asked Kesselring. 'The island girls are getting a little stale for you now, eh?'

Nikki Jagmann grinned, neither confirming nor denying the truth, although Kesselring's weak joke had served its purpose, and the men felt more at ease, now that they had some inkling of what was in store for them. In truth von Schellenberg need not have worried about how they would react to the news of the four dead paratroopers who, as prisoners in Granville, had enjoyed a much healthier diet than the 28,000 soldiers trapped in the islands. At least the Americans fed their prisoners well, whereas over the last few weeks there had been a public outcry in Jersey about the number of pets which were going missing, taken, the Kommandant knew, by hungry soldiers supplementing their rations with any meat they could find.

'You were right about the cargo boats,' said von Schellenberg, picking up a thin bamboo cane from his desk and pointing to the harbour area. 'Because the ports of St Malo and Cherbourg have become dangerous to shipping, the Anglo-Americans are having to use smaller ports, like Granville, to unload their coal, a commodity that we, too, desperately need, as well as food and medical supplies. Each day at least one collier arrives from Wales, skirting the islands and approaching the coast from the north, keeping well away from our big guns in Alderney. Notice – here – the two gunboats which are protecting the colliers and – here – the barracks, home before the war to over 300 French servicemen. The French have maintained a garrison there, but we don't believe there are more than 30 or 40 infantrymen, ein Schutzenzug, in residence.' Von Schellenberg pointed first to the outer harbour walls, and then to a large, rectangular building, overlooking the port, to the north-west of the town.

It was Jagmann who spotted the Americans. To the east of the barracks and nestling in a crook of land overlooking the northern beaches was an impressive hotel, dominating the coastal skyline. The Hotel Normandie.

'The American flag,' he said. 'So presumably that is the headquarters of the American general.' He paused.

'Damn Yankees,' he continued, without real venom, but saying what he'd thought for a long time aloud. 'Without their interference this war would have been over two years ago.'

None of the other officers needed to voice their agreement, but tacit approval could be seen in their eyes and in Lindenheim's brief nod in Jagmann's direction.

It was at this stage of the proceedings that von Schellenberg decided it was as good a time as any to reveal the real purpose of this crazy mission to attack the allies even as the rest of the mighty German army was withdrawing from occupied Europe. He knew he must take these men into his confidence, hoping they would remain loyal to his leadership and hoping they would not interpret his words as a criticism of Adolf Hitler, who refused, point-blank, to admit the possibility of defeat.

'You are correct,' he said. 'The war would be ours – even now – if the Americans weren't fighting. But they are in Europe and we, despite controlling these islands, are cut off from the Fatherland because they, and the British, are overrunning France.

'Perhaps we have tried to fight against too many enemies on too many fronts. But of one thing I am convinced, as we sit here and pretend that our armies will somehow stem this tide, and that is that we will not win this war.'

Von Schellenberg straightened his back and looked directly at each of the men in turn. He had weighed his words carefully, knowing that such an admission was tantamount to treason, and while he knew he could trust Hoffmeister implicitly he couldn't help wondering if Hoffmeister's trust in these four soldiers was equally justified. In particular he looked at von Bastion – such a complex personality, who, despite the pasty colour of his skin, was a superb athlete, a keep-fit fanatic whose health and strength were a tribute to one of the more endearing philosophies of the Hitler Youth. Such a blunt dismissal of the past six or seven years of his life might not be taken kindly by the young officer, but, thoughtful and quiet, he had not been provoked to any violent objection. Instead he was waiting for more information – an outline of the action he had been promised. So von Schellenberg, with cold deliberation, repeated his words.

'We will not and cannot win this war. But . . .' and again he paused, hoping the next few minutes would see his words sink in deeply enough to make their mark, '. . . we can hold the Allies to ransom. We can negotiate from a position of strength. And the key to our impact on what is happening in France lies here, at the Hotel Normandie.'

As he tapped the model of the hotel lightly with the cane, Hoffmeister noticed, to his surprise, that the General's left hand was clenched tightly by his side, betraying to his friend all the deep-felt emotion he'd been storing up, waiting to be released as all the scheming, all the preparation, all the anxious hours he had spent devising this plan were put to the test. Von Schellenberg was willing these men to join him in his quest for glory; willing them to go out and do the impossible; to capture this small French town and to bring him home the greatest prize of all.

His voice rose a little, beguiling, demanding: 'By taking General Eisenhower prisoner, by bringing him back to our island fortress, we have a means of negotiating peace on our terms, not theirs. Here, in this seaside hotel, is the one man who can order the fighting to stop; the one man we can hold to ransom, knowing that with him in our power, our enemies cannot – will not – ignore our demands. If we truly care about the Fatherland we must not let them bleed it dry. Gentlemen, with this man, with this one pug-faced general in our hands I believe we can shape the end of the war as we would wish it to be.'

By now the General's voice, previously crisp and clipped, with little passion, had risen to a level of heightened emotion which didn't go unnoticed by the men sitting in front of him.

Von Schellenberg paused for a moment or two to allow them to dwell on the audacity of such a plan.

They all knew of this American, who had helped turn the tide of war against them in North Africa and Italy. And just as they were left in no doubt about the sincerity of von Schellenberg's words, so no-one doubted the impact it would have on the rest of the world if Dwight D Eisenhower were taken prisoner. Certainly it would be a shattering blow against the Allies – wasn't he the most senior general of all, in complete control of the Anglo-American push from the west? Capture him, hold him to ransom here in the islands, and then let the rest of the world knock on their door, as they negotiated the end of hostilities from a position of strength.

This day, 24 February, 1945, would be etched in von Schellenberg's memory forever. He was offering his men the opportunity to make history: if the war wouldn't come to Jersey, he would take the war to France, and in such a way that the Anglo-Americans would be forced to listen to his demands for peace.

'And if we take him, do you not believe that the Americans would try everything in their power to take him back?' asked Nikki, innocently, as if the Kommandant hadn't considered they would dare to do such a thing.

'They will not attack us to take him back,' von Schellenberg said, smiling. 'Do not think that I am naïve enough to believe that our German fortifications have frightened the enemy away from these islands for so long. I am more of a realist than that. They do not want to fight in the islands because there are 43,000 other hardy souls living here. And they are all British. Do you really think they would launch an all-out attack, just for one man, with so many other lives at stake?

'Imagine. 43,000 – and one. Eisenhower. Not even a Britisher – But an American! And an American who could negotiate on our behalf directly with the president of the USA.

'The Americans are the real puppet-masters in this final stage of war. They hold the purse strings. They will want to control the peace. They are afraid and suspicious of the Russians and their communist intent, and will be much easier to deal with than the British, who will want to make our countrymen squeal loudly, like pigs. Steal me a general, gentlemen; that is all I am asking you to do. Steal me a general and bring him to me.'

Von Schellenberg banged his hand down once, hard, on the cluttered desk where he had planned most of the Granville raid. If he could imbue these men with his own enthusiasm for the Granville raid it would be a success. If he could not, then the failure would probably cost him his life.

'For four long years I have been rotting here, in what has become, for me, a pretend war – a war in which I administer justice to islanders whose main concern is that a neighbour has stolen a rabbit, or that a soldier has not saluted before searching a house for contraband.

'This is not war; it is child-minding. Child-minding and petty bureaucracy! It is a job I have been instructed to do. But I am a soldier. I joined the army expecting to fight – and it is this fight which I am bequeathing to you.

'Starting from tomorrow you will train to take and hold Granville for as long as it takes to steal every large cargo ship you can; to sink or destroy the rest; to blow up all the portside defences; and to bring back to the islands all the VIP officers living here – in the Hotel Normandie, and here – in the Hotel des Ormes, where other American troops are based. You will train your men to work efficiently, effectively, and you will hammer home the message that one careless moment by any of the men under your command could turn a well-rehearsed victory into a disorganised rout.

'But I insist, gentlemen, that you do not reveal the purpose of this plan to anyone outside the four walls of this room, not until the time is right for you to do so. The fewer people who know of our plans, the better. We cannot afford the rest of the island to learn what we intend to do, and you are all well aware that too frequently in the past islanders have taken it into their heads to try to escape from Jersey and to report back to British Intelligence in London.

'You will have three weeks to choose your men, and to train them, and at the end of those three weeks you, and they, will know every nook and cranny of the town, from the cobbled streets to the ebb and flow of the sea. If you do not, or if you do not believe you will succeed, you will not go. Accomplish this task and the Führer and the German people will praise and reward you. Fail and you would best be served by staying where you will find yourselves in early March – in enemy France.'

The Kommandant's tone was authoritative, urgent; the passion remained, but was under careful control. He could not afford to let any member of the group leave the room without realising the importance he ascribed to this raid, nor his demand for total loyalty from all those who would take part. He had not lied to these men, nor would he keep anything back he believed they should know. Such honesty made him vulnerable but, by the same token, they must realise that they owed him a debt of gratitude for taking them into his confidence and choosing them, above all others, to lead the Granville raid.

The perfunctory 'any questions?' which followed was not a request as such. It was an indication that, for now, the meeting was coming to an end, although they knew von Schellenberg's style well enough to know that later he would see each man in turn to go through every detail of the raid, as it affected them.

Von Bastion, the youngest of the five, spoke.

'You say we will lose the war Herr General, but in the next breath you say we must attack our enemies and take one of them hostage, to allow us to "negotiate", you say.' He paused, a little uncomfortable about the question he wanted to ask. 'But the Führer. Surely he will never agree to such negotiation . . .'

It was a question that had to be asked. Von Schellenberg knew that, and accepted its importance, for if it were not answered now it could cause problems later.

From his own point of view it posed another, potentially much more deadly question. Once answered, would these five men show allegiance to him, or judge his words as those of a traitor, words which should immediately be conveyed back to Hitler in his bunker in Berlin? Perhaps there was a more important allegiance they had to realise, as the war moved towards its irrevocable end.

'If the raid is only a partial success,' von Schellenberg said, choosing his words slowly, deliberately. 'If you sink the ships but don't capture them. If you fail to take any prisoners but blow up a military installation or two, all of your successes will be conveyed quickly to the Fatherland where they will appear like manna from heaven. Hemmed in on all sides, our people need to know that from deep inside enemy-held territory we are still capable of battle, that we can still wound our enemy as our armies regroup, preparing themselves to fight back. The Führer, I have no doubt, will turn any small success into the illusion of hope. Anything more than a small success, and you will find yourselves fêted as heroes.

'And, if during the raid you *do* capture the American general, he won't be wasted, either by Island Command or by the Führer. What I have set before you is the truth, as I see it. And at some stage I would expect the Führer to accept that truth, too. Perhaps he already has, and with Eisenhower as our prisoner he will finally admit it to us, and to our people.' He faltered slightly, betraying more of the emotion which he had so carefully bottled up for so very long.

'But we will not know how the Führer will treat this hypothetical problem until we – no, not we – *you* have turned it from an idea into reality. That will be your task, gentleman, not mine.'

Von Schellenberg looked around the white-walled room; at the desk, at the maps on the wall, at the large model of the seaside town he knew by heart, and finally at the men. He did not want them to feel part of some hidden conspiracy but if they did, and if any Brutus lay hidden among them, he would know soon enough.

It was a risk he had to take; and with Vice-admiral Kreiser sniffing arrogantly in the wings, waiting to ram the dagger home, he might have been best served by idling away the rest of the war doing nothing but waiting, until, inevitably, Berlin fell. But it wasn't in his nature to sit idly by and let a chance like this go begging. If he was penalised for showing initiative, then so be it. The risk was all his; but at least these men now had his confidence, and it was a relief to discover that they didn't seem unduly perturbed by the task he'd set them. In particular he was relieved that Otto von Bastion appeared happier, believing that at long last he could earn the glory he craved and that he would be a hero back home.

Nikki Jagmann seemed slightly amused at the earnest way that the youngster had asked the question, while Lindenheim was undoubtedly grateful to have been chosen but saw it more as a tribute to his professionalism and his meticulous attention to detail. An order was an order; he didn't care about the politics of war, he merely did what he was told to do and let his superior officers guide his conscience.

Both Kesselring and Hoffmeister, the older, more experienced members of the five-man team, understood the hidden dangers of accepting von Schellenberg's command. But both, in their own way, trusted him – they certainly had much more faith in their Kommandant than they did in that zealot Kreiser, who would sacrifice his own mother in exchange for a congratulations telegram from the Führer's bunker. As long as the men under their command weren't placed in impossible danger they would go along with their commanding officer, knowing that he had their interests at heart.

'Any more questions?' Von Schellenberg said, placing the cane on the desk, ready to leave the meeting in the capable hands of Hoffmeister.

'What if this General Eisenhower doesn't want to come quietly – what if he resists or, if the worse comes to the worse, if we can't. . .' Nikki coughed, looking for the right word. 'What happens if we can't persuade this man amicably that he might enjoy a boat ride to Jersey – for the good of his health.'

Von Schellenberg had already considered the question and had decided on the answer many days before.

'Drug him if you have to. Carry him screaming if you have to, but get him here. That's all I ask of you. Get him here.' The Kommandant's voice had regained its hard edge, leaving them in no doubt that he expected them to obey this, the most important command.

'Any more questions? No?' Von Schellenberg nodded. 'Good. From now on, until I see each of you individually, and until my final briefing, Colonel Hoffmeister will be in charge. He has my complete confidence and I ask you to share your confidences, and your questions, with him. He will be leading you into battle, although the success of this raid rests on all of you working together.

'I want no heroics: success, in war, comes through co-operation and by gaining, and keeping, the upper hand. The more you prepare for this battle, the better. The more you come to know this seaside town, the better. The more carefully you pick your men, the better. Attention to detail, and making certain that everyone plays a full part in the Granville raid will ensure its success. Be assured I cannot contemplate failure. And now, I am afraid, I have more form-filling and written reports to attend to. Later, much later, I will see you again, but for now I leave you in the capable hands of Colonel Hoffmeister. Do not disappoint me. Heil Hitler.'

With a sharp clicking of heels, accompanied by a similarly

sharp raising of the right arm, he left the room, tall, proud, patriotic. Only the small bamboo cane remained on the edge of the desk, where he had placed it a minute before.

As Nikki Jagmann stretched his legs in front of him, wondering idly what his part would be in this raid on France, the cane took on another guise. It became a symbol of obedience, as if the headmaster had left it there to remind his students that he would eventually be back, and expected no trouble in class while he was gone.

4

Practice run

THE Emerald Hotel at Bagatelle, on the outskirts of St Helier, the island's capital, was a large, predominantly white building. A functional hotel, it had been built too quickly and too efficiently to have any personality; it had nevertheless been one of the top hotels in the Island before the war. Indeed, even during the so-called Phoney War of April and May, 1940, when both sides were arming and re-arming as quickly as they could ready for the real thing to follow, it had played host to hundreds of visitors from Britain, some of them making the most of the last days of sun and sand they would ever know.

But on 28 June, 1940, the Phoney War became a real war as the Germans arrived, announcing their presence in Jersey by first bombing the harbour in the mistaken belief that queues of lorries waiting to unload their many sacks of potatoes bound for England were carrying British troops. This mistake had cost the Island nine lives, including that of retired postman Philip Couilliard, who spotted two planes travelling low and fast and coming in from the sea at La Rocque, on the east coast. He was crossing the road from his house to the beach at the time, and never imagined, in the early afternoon sunshine, that one of these two specks on the horizon was bringing him death. Even as it turned low, and flew directly over his head he never thought of diving for cover. Philip Couilliard, the 66-year-old retired postman, was dead even before the plane banked sharply away, cut to pieces in a hail of tracer fire. The only mercy that the pilot had shown was to make it quick as he flew over the built-up St Clement coastline to Havre des Pas in the south, and to the harbour. Philip Couilliard was the first casualty of the war in Jersey, but with four long years of Occupation to go, he was not going to be the last.

The two German fighters, reunited in the air, took it in turn to strafe warehouses, potato lorries and anyone foolish enough to emerge from cover to see what was happening. There was no answering fire – there couldn't be, for the island had been demilitarised – and the pilots later laughed and joked with each other as they described how first one and then the other had sent the island's inhabitants running for cover, particularly one old farmworker who, slower than the rest, had almost danced his way to safety behind a packing shed . . . almost, but not quite, for when the pilots turned their planes back to base the old man lay where he had fallen, his body reddening in the dust.

The pilots' account of the raid told the Wehrmacht in Cherbourg what they wanted to believe but, until that day, couldn't believe without fear that they were being drawn into a trap. The Channel Islands were undefended and ripe for plucking. With no British troops and no weapons to defend themselves, the authorities in Guernsey, Jersey, Sark and Alderney had no option but to surrender, which Jersey did on 1 July, by painting a large white crosses in the Royal Square and at the airport. Within a matter of hours the island was occupied and within a matter of weeks the Germans had billeted themselves in hotels, schools and in all the better houses.

One of the hotels they first commandeered was the Emerald, which was first used as a communications centre and then as a training school.

The main hotel was four storeys high, with a flat roof, sea views from the second and third floors, sixty bedrooms and an annex. The annex, only six years old, contained another twenty-four bedrooms. These were a temporary home for the officers and most of the men who would be landed in France in 'Operation Fahrmann' – Operation Ferryman – the name given to the attack on Granville by Colonel Hoffmeister.

The Emerald was a spacious hotel, appreciated by men used to living in much humbler surroundings, but comfort was not the reason why it – called the Taubenschlag, or dovecote, by the men because of the rounded windows at the back – had been chosen. For the next three weeks it would represent the Hotel Normandie and for the next three weeks no islander was allowed within a quarter of a mile of the place, or to talk to its army inhabitants, in case they got wind of what was happening, and smuggled news of the intended raid out of the island.

* * * *

28 February: A clear but cool day with the occasional high cloud scudding across the skies and a chill wind blowing in from the east.

Eight hundred yards from the hotel fifty men, all in uniform, are running, running as if the devil is a yard behind them. One man – the leader – dives across the courtyard, machine gun tucked beneath his arm, the safety catch off and the barrel pointing low. He moves to the last window of the main building on the eastern side and smashes his gun through the pane of glass. Korporal Bruegel, giving cover against imaginary resistance, follows. These are the first men through. But as in a game of catch-me-if-you-can, they have been given a five second start. The other men have been ordered to make up this brief delay, to earn for themselves the right to take the front man's place. Always a race against time. If you're too slow, someone else takes over. This is the third run today but only the first in which the hotel window is broken and the entire hotel is taken.

Meanwhile, to the rear, the men of Jagmann's group use grappling irons and rope to swarm up to the third floor of the Taubenschlag, knowing that they have been given fifty seconds to make the climb and find a way in.

Over thirty seconds have passed. All of the men feel that this, at last, is real training for war. There is a camaraderie of urgency as they clamber in. Bruegel and the officer in front of him, Oberleutnant Kern, are by now pushing their way through to the large restaurant area downstairs. They know the place well enough to count their way past the tables and desks as they wade through the darkness. This is the map room, which will be thoroughly searched and where, perhaps, they will find the General.

By now Jagmann and his men have taken the back of the hotel, combing every room as they go, moving forwards and downwards so that no occupant, awake or asleep, is allowed the opportunity to resist. Over four minutes have elapsed, and only a few rooms remain. The hotel is alive with black-faced, nervously excited commandos, ready to kill if necessary with fingers itching to pull the triggers of real guns loaded with real bullets. They enjoy the game hugely, and within the space of just over six and a half minutes the hotel, to all intents and purposes, is theirs.

Upstairs Jagmann is in complete control. At the first floor windows he has posted sentries, with guns pointing downwards at anyone foolish enough to wander in through the front door. With at least four men on every floor, covering every entrance and exit, the raiding party has done its job well. Or so the raiding party believes.

In the map room four soldiers stand guard as Bruegel and Kern throw open desks and drawers, stuffing anything that could be of military importance into two large water-tight suitcases. Quantity, not quality, will be their byword on the day of the raid simply because they have no spare time to read through all the files and papers they hope to find. Meanwhile, as 'hostages' are herded together in a corner somewhere else in the hotel, the 'Boy', the chubby-faced explosives expert Thomas Schmidt, whistles to himself tunelessly as he always does when he's lost in his work and sets a fuse.

This, he knows, is not the real thing. There are too many

other attacks to be made, too many other dummy raids on the Emerald Hotel before they will allow real fuses to be set, for although he knows his job well and believes he can make the Hotel Normandie fold like a pack of cards, an accident now could jeopardise the expedition and endanger the lives of up to forty men who have no intention of dying on enemy soil.

Later on the the fuses will be set for real; but the only time they will be properly set will be in a French hotel on Saturday, 9 March, at about 2.40 am – if all goes according to plan.

The last charge in place, the Boy is still whistling. A little jauntier now that he knows he has finished his work for the evening, he makes his way to the map-room/restaurant where the prisoners are still huddled in a corner, and where the search for documents is coming to an end.

'All finished, chief,' he says, knowing that they need his expertise too badly to grumble about the informality of his language.

'Within' – and he looks at his watch – 'within the next tweleve minutes, I reckon, the place will go up like a tinder box.'

Five minutes later, he, Bruegel and Kern, propelling another man as 'hostage' in front of them through the front door, are on their way back to the imaginary shoreline below. A little way behind, in the middle of the group, Nikki Jagmann staggers slightly under the weight of the contents of a large sack slung heavily over his left shoulder. In three weeks time it could be anything from a sack of coal to a VIP American general. The raiding party fans out, some of the soldiers ready to give covering fire to Jagmann, Bruegel, Kern and their prisoners, the others already some way in front of the party, prepared to open fire at the drop of a hat. Twenty-three minutes have passed, discounting the thirty-minute delay they have allowed for their approach to the beaches from the sea. By the time the last man has scrambled back over the small granite wall designated as safety, the raiding party is at least two minutes clear of the Boy's twelve-minute warning.

The soldiers seem happy, conscious that they are well inside the two hours they will have from the moment they leave their ship to the moment they return. And if they can take the hotel like this, capturing it in less than seven minutes and ransacking it effectively in under half an hour, then nothing will go wrong.

But it is not good enough.

'Six minutes THIRTY-SIX SECONDS!' bellows Hoffmeister as the men gather around him in the clearing. Apart from the light from their torches and the occasional blast from the woods, all they can see is his silhouette, massive in the night, black and foreboding. It is 2.30 in the morning and the Colonel is outraged. 'Thirty six seconds more than we have allowed you to capture the hotel. And Hoffmann. You could be heard 200 yards away with your cough. Schuster – if you want to go to the party you must learn to keep your big arse down – unless you want it shot to pieces. Von Brauchitsch: when you shoulder charge a door, be positive. Three times you gave it a gentle tap, as if you were knocking on it, to see if anyone was in. Three times you failed to break it open, by which time, if there'd been anyone within, they'd be sitting up in bed quite calmly waiting to fill you full of holes on your fourth attempt. You weigh – what – about 110 kilos?' Klaus von Brauchitsch nods. 'Then *use* it: don't namby-pamby your way in worrying about your poor shoulder when there are six or seven men's lives at stake behind you.'

The men, including the bulky Klaus von Brauchitsch, accept their leader's criticism without complaint. They believe they did well. Their Oberstleutnant, however, wants it doing better. Not because he is a petty tyrant, who can't be satisfied no matter how well they do, but because he wants the raid to be carried out to perfection. And because, they like to think, he doesn't want any of them to end up being killed unnecessarily.

5

A letter received

THE following day, the first rehearsal to bring three boats into St Helier harbour with no lights showing, to board three vessels designated as 'enemy' and to take aim against portside installations was nothing less than a disaster. Instead of taking twenty minutes to manoeuvre the boats into position it had taken nearly an hour, and besides the shouting and cursing as different instructions had been yelled and counter-yelled as they attempted to squeeze the ships through the narrow harbour entrance, one man had fallen overboard and another had been knocked senseless when running too quickly and carelessly along the decks.

It was not going to plan, and when von Schellenberg heard the news he had grave doubts that the combined land operation and the sea operation could go ahead without more serious consequences that would inevitably cost his men their lives. Although he had stepped back from Operation Fahrmann to allow Hoffmeister and his four senior officers the opportunity to turn the outline plan into something they could mould and shape into a coherent whole, the raid worried him. He wanted – needed – so much for it to be a success.

And then, in the middle of his vital preparations for what was to be a first taste of war for many of his men, there came a letter which tested his commitment to his homeland in a most terrible way.

Dearest Pieter,

Know, first of all, that I love you dearly, even though we are so many miles apart. Know, too, that I am still alive and looking forward to the day when you and I can be together again, once this awful war is over.

They have arrested me – but you know that. You also know that my brother, Stefan, believed that the Fatherland would be served best if the Führer should die. Where he is now I do not know, although I have heard one rumour that they have already killed him.

I heard that story from one of the men who came to our house just over a week ago insisting that I knew of this plot to kill the little Austrian, and that I would be punished if I did not tell him everything I knew. But knowing nothing, what could I tell him? That I, too, was a traitor? He left after three hours but he told me he would return.

He did so three nights ago, with another man, and brought me here, to a prison in Vilseck. From my cell I can hear the sparrows singing quite cheerfully in the morning, but I cannot see them, for the only window is a tiny one, high up in the wall. In their happiness I can take some consolation that at least the world outside remains the same while my own small world has been turned upside down. I have told the truth, constantly – that I knew nothing of the plot until my brother was arrested. But they are not convinced, and every time they ask me questions they bring in your name. I tell them you are a loyal Deutchslander, but that is not enough. 'Loyal to the Führer?' They ask. 'Or loyal only to my brother and family?'

They try to confuse me, to trap me, asking me questions over and over again. They do not hit me or beat me, just this constant asking of questions, again and again and again, sometimes late at night until the dawn when they suddenly change, ask me to forgive them, say they are 'merely doing their job', before bowing, and leaving the room. Then, within an hour, they return and question me again. Always the same questions, and only my love for you, and the sound of the sparrows to keep me sane.

I do not know if you, too, knew of this threat to Herr Hitler. I tell them that you are a good German; but that does not satisfy them.

They allow me only one visitor – my father – to whom I entrust this secret letter. I am in good health although not without fear; not for myself, but for you, my husband, for I fear deeply for your safety. Do not worry for me but please, dear, dear Pieter. Choose your enemies wisely; much more wisely than poor brother Stefan.

All of this I presume you can find out from High Command or your uncle. But I write to tell you, my dear husband, that although they would want to blacken your name just as they have tried to blacken mine, they cannot succeed. I will not give them the 'proof' they need to arrest you, or to destroy my brother, wherever he may be and whether or not he is still alive.

In these terrible times a songbird and my love for you keep me sane; just as the memories I have of those nights we spent curled up at home in front of a log fire, the two of us together, no need for words as our thoughts entwined, give me hope for the future. We will survive the war, my husband, you and I, for I will live for you as I know you will live for me.

I love you, my fine, handsome soldier husband,

and hope that this letter will give you some faith in our war against a common enemy – bullies, lies, and our own 'dear' Führer. That horrid little man! I pray for your safety and trust in truth and God.

Sleep safely in my love tonight,
Marte

Von Schellenberg read the letter again, and continued to look at it, without seeing a thing. Marte did not know that he had known of Stauffenberg's bungled attempt to kill Hitler, and that he had tacitly approved. But why should she know? He would never tell her anything that might lead to her death, although he knew that she might well have suspected he was somehow involved. As long as they didn't hurt her – that was the main thing . . . not hurting her, no matter what they did to him or poor Stefan Bonheiffer, his brother-in-law.

A noise in the outer office brought von Schellenberg back to the reality of the moment. He shook his head very quickly from side to side to clear his mind, and then put the letter on the only ashtray in the room, lighting two corners with the help of a clumsy pocket cigarette lighter. As the flames caught hold, he told himself that if she would survive for him, then he, too, would survive for her. She was ten years younger than he; not physically tough but mentally very strong; slight but good looking with a stubborn streak in her which would turn to a thin-lipped look as she grew older. If she grew older . . .

He knew that if they weren't satisfied with her replies it was only a matter of time before they asked – demanded – the off-the-record chat with him, with Kreiser waiting to denounce him if there was the merest hint that he had spoken against the Führer. All of this, however, was yet to come. For the moment at least von Schellenberg had control of his own destiny, and the destiny of these tiny islands.

Marte's letter curled and flickered into one last blaze of life and then subsided into black nothingness. As the island

Kommandant pulled a wastebasket over to the desk and was carefully spilling the ashes into it, the door opened and in walked Kreiser, not renowned as a respecter of niceties.

6

Choose your enemies

'SORRY to hear about your wife,' said Kreiser, as if he had been reading every thought in von Schellenberg's head for the past ten minutes.

Von Schellenberg started. That Kreiser knew so much, so fully . . . He looked at the Vice-admiral, an implacable enemy, whose bullying ways had been well-learned in one of Hitler's élite training schools. He was a product of the long-winded Nationalsozialistiche Führungsstab der Kriegsmarine, which assured its students that just as it was Germany's destiny to control the western world, so it was Adolf Hitler's destiny to become that world's natural leader.

Kreiser had proved an excellent student; he possessed no subtlety of thought and, when told that it was his duty to become part of a new Teutonic order, he accepted that duty without equivocation. Similarly, when Herr Hitler addressed the nation, telling his people that they would win the war, Kreiser saw it as his patriotic duty to fight to the last until it was won. He was a man whose courage on behalf of the Führer was unquestionable, and he had already proved his bravery not once but three times, by running the gauntlet of British gunboats to bring wounded soldiers safely out of St Malo in August, 1944, when the Allies began their siege of the town.

Sadly, the heroic rearguard action by Colonel von Aulock

in St Malo was in vain, and under sustained heavy artillery fire and against overwhelming odds the sensible decision would have been to sue for peace. Hitler, however, ordered otherwise. The siege continued, and for every casualty Kreiser's small fleet of rescue ships took on board, and ferried back to Jersey, five men died defending the indefensible. It was 17 August, a full three days after Hitler had ordered von Aulock to fight to the very last man, that the end came and the fighting stopped.

As St Malo was a coastal town in western France, and the Allies were already making vast strides east, towards the Franco-German border, its bloody defence made no more sense than a fleabite to the all-powerful Anglo-American army. For his bravery in rescuing so many wounded soldiers in the face of heavy enemy fire Ernst Kreiser was awarded the Knight's Cross. For sacrificing so many men in defence of the town Colonel von Aulock was awarded the Oak Leaves to add to the Knight's Cross he'd already won. Meanwhile, several hundred men were unnecessarily dead and the old walled town of St Malo lay in ruins.

Afterwards, even though he had seen, at first hand, St Malo being taken and knew that the Allies were moving quickly eastwards through France, Vice-admiral Kreiser refused to accept that the war was lost. Nothing, it seemed, could shake his faith in the Führer's ability to work miracles. His belief was so unshakeable that von Schellenberg often wondered whether this belief, and Kreiser's undoubted courage, weren't merely an indication that he lacked imagination. Perhaps Kreiser could not envisage losing; perhaps he could not imagine the carnage and devastation that fighting against impossible odds, until the last man under his command was dead, could bring.

And what of Kreiser? What were his views of the island, and the men under von Schellenberg's command?

He may have had faith in his own Marinekorps and treated them well, but he was dismissive of the 619 Division under von Schellenberg's command, complaining that they marched poorly and were over-friendly with the islanders.

He was dismissive, too, of the islanders, who had nicknamed him Captain Hook. His slick-backed grey hair, short at the sides and thick on top, his high, receding forehead and his black, hooded eyebrows gave him, from his eyebrows upwards, the look of a bird of prey. Beneath the eyebrows a bulbous nose above fleshy lips gave him the look of a thick-jowled pirate, and always, when in the public eye, he wore his Vice-admiral's dark blue uniform. He dressed immaculately and combed his hair back for effect; for without hairstyle and uniform he was simply a tubby man, of middle height with a cruel face and tiny, piercing eyes which rarely showed affection.

If ever he had learned of the islanders' nickname – which he didn't – he would not have worried. He was not interested in their petty word games; his single-minded ambition was to control not only the navy in island waters, but also the destiny of every man, woman and child living on the island itself. Power was his one, over-riding ambition in life, and if the quest for this commodity meant pushing von Schellenberg to one side to find it, then so be it. He saw himself as a hero of the Third Reich, and as long as he had his moment of glory, which he believed would come when he refused to surrender the islands, he would be happy.

People were merely pawns to men like Kreiser, and von Schellenberg, who had seen many ambitious officers like him over the past thirty years, had learned to tolerate them without ever learning to like them. They made implacable enemies and insufferable friends, whose one common ambition was to get to play God. Von Schellenberg shook his head. In the past he had friends on his side; friends of intellect in the German High Command who would not have allowed a man like Kreiser to be given more than the hint of power; friends who had the capacity to deflate such bullying creatures, who knew how dangerous they were becoming but were capable of laughing at their pomposity. But here, in Jersey, it would seem that the two most important men in the islands – he and Kreiser – were on a collision course – with Kreiser's star in the ascendancy just as his own was dwindling rapidly as his friendship with those who would kill the Führer became common knowledge back home. Kreiser had Hitler's ear – he was sure of that – while he . . . all he had was a crazy dream about kidnapping an American general, and a wife who, even now, might be selling her husband to the SS for a momentary respite from their incessant questioning.

Ah well, he had looked after his men and the islands as best he could for the past three years and he would not hand either over to Kreiser without a struggle, even though he knew that there would be more battles ahead. For six generations the von Schellenberg family had served their Fatherland and he would not let this upstart ruin his family name without putting up a damn good fight first.

'Good morning, Herr General,' said the Vice-admiral, clicking his heels and saluting.

Von Schellenberg glanced up at him, briefly, before looking down again at some papers on his desk, giving the impression that the paperwork was much more important than the man standing in front of him. He chose to ignore for a moment the Vice-admiral's outstretched arm, a salute which wouldn't have been out of place on a naval parade ground. Then, having acknowledged it with a less than courteous salute of his own, he began to speak: lounging back in his chair as he did so, knowing full well that such a relaxed attitude would gall the other officer tremendously.

'Kreiser,' he said. 'Kreiser, between you and me, tell me. What is it about me that you so intensely dislike?'

Kreiser puffed himself up. He was a stocky figure who, despite loving a uniform, wore it badly. 'Sir, I believe we should set more of an example with these islanders when they tell our men that they will lose the war.

'It does our war effort no good at all. And the sloppiness in the way the men march off duty. They walk as if they believe in our defeat and dress as if they had just said goodbye to the brothel. They no longer parade as if they were Germans, and as Befehlshaber of the Channel Islands it is your duty to ensure . . .'

'Yes, yes, yes,' said von Schellenberg testily. 'We will return to that later. But I will repeat again. Why do you wish to undermine my authority? Why?'

There was barely a pause before Kreiser continued in similar vein, ignoring the question and offering advice of his own.

'I believe if we court-martial the next soldier who suggests we will not win, in what must only be a temporary hiccup before the Führer launches his new secret weapon, the V2 rockets . . .'

'Well I'll tell you why,' said the General, looking directly into the unblinking face of the man before him. 'I'll tell you why. You hate me because I was born to command. You had to earn it. And because you want the war to continue long enough to give you more power than you have ever known in your life. Power to do whatever you might wish with these island people, power until you are either the Führer's pet lapdog or dead.

'And you hate me because I am an obstacle to this impossible dream you have, a dream which will turn the island into a battlefield if you have your way, a dream that will become a living nightmare not for you – your sort will always survive – but for thousands of good men of either side who are stranded here, powerless, because the war has passed them by.

'Of course you hate me most because I am the last obstacle to your ambitions. Isn't that right, Herr Kreiser?

'Isn't it right that you would stab me in the back tomorrow if you felt it would earn you another notch up the ladder – stab me in the back without feeling an ounce of remorse. Isn't that right, Vice-admiral Kreiser?'

All the humour, all the banter had gone from von Schellenberg's voice, to be replaced by a hard edge he knew the other man would despise because all he said was true. He hated himself for the bitterness he had displayed, showing the open wound he knew was festering between them. But if he could only make this pig-headed Schwein Pachter react to his words he would feel it had been worth it.

'Tell me what I already know, Kreiser. Tell me what I know so, so well, about your intense hatred for my family, for my background, for my standing in your way as you seek control of this isle.

'Tell me, now, before I order you out to some lowly task. To cleaning the latrines, perhaps; to standing night duty in some lonely corner in some god-forsaken corner of the island. Just tell me, Kreiser; empty your soul of some of that malice you've been storing up these last six months. SHOW ME YOUR HATE, man. We both know it's there, not far beneath the surface.'

If it had been rehearsed it couldn't have been better. In a fine blend of weary resignation and scoffing anger, von Schellenberg's showed his contempt for a thick-set brute of a man whose presence he found unbearable.

But the Vice-admiral stood his ground, and even allowed a little smile to play on his lips as if he were conducting this interview, not the Kommandant.

For a moment the two men were locked in almost total silence; a silence exaggerated for both by the loud tick-tocking of a clock (Sheffield-made, from before the war) on the wall. As if beating time to the inner rage of both men, it filled the hostile vacuum that existed in the few feet separating them.

As von Schellenberg paused, wondering what effect, if any, his words would have on this implacable foe, it was Kreiser who spoke first, in a silky undertone, as if to a child who hadn't yet realised that he lived in an adults' world.

'I will take leave of you until this afternoon, Herr General, and I will come back when you are more in control. A German officer, you know, should always be in control, in every situation. Even in death.'

And he saluted, quickly this time, before turning his back and striding out on surprisingly light feet.

As the younger man left the room, quietly, without fuss, not bothering to turn to see what effect his mild reproach had had on the island Kommandant, in von Schellenberg's mind the same words kept ticking away like some kind of ready-to-detonate time-bomb.

'Choose your enemies wisely,' his wife's letter had said. 'Choose your enemies wisely . . .'

7

Calm before the storm

IT was Saturday evening. In the large restaurant area of the Emerald Hotel the atmosphere was very different to that which had prevailed in the island for many months before. The men who were living here, preparing for Operation Fahrmann, or Operation Kohlesack as some of them had laughingly called it – the coalsack referring to the large bag Nikki Jagmann had been seen dragging from the hotel – enjoyed a kind of gleeful excitement that at last they were preparing for battle, and with these preparations came the knowledge that they had been hand-picked for the adventure to come.

Most of the men had now gone to their rooms (with no alcohol and only sparse rations to live on since the islands had been cut off from the rest of the world, there was no enjoyment in staying up late), although a small group of nine men remained. These did have alcohol, courtesy of Jagmann, who had confiscated two half-bottles of spirits he'd found in an old Jerseyman's garden. It had been the newly-turned soil which had given the game away; newly-turned in a piece of scrubland that bore neither fruit nor flower. Though little enough shared between the nine of them, the rum and whisky had proved sufficient to add an air of jollity to the night's proceedings.

'French. Such a small woman I thought she would break in two, but once inside I found there was oceans of room.' The Lieutenant pinched middle finger and thumb together, to make a circle.

'And her skin would have been so much nicer to touch if only her breath hadn't reminded me of cabbage. That, and the smell of fish . . .'

There was a general round of laughter.

'Still,' Nikki sighed, almost apologetically, 'it had to be done, I suppose.'

'But a 15-year-old . . .' said one of the other men.

'No,' said Nick. 'Fifteen going on forty-five. An old maid by twenty. I know my women.'

'But do you have to sleep with every woman you meet?' the other soldier asked, half envious, half curious at Nikki's constant desire for sex.

'No,' said Nikki. 'No, it's not compulsory. But they beg me to – honestly they do – and they offer it to me for free.

'I don't have to queue outside the brothel at Grève d'Azette, checking myself afterwards that I'm not diseased. I know where my women have been; and although I might not be the first, I haven't had to follow some pimply youth who goes red in the face and stutters as he undoes his flies . . .'

His sly grin towards Thomas Schmidt, sitting towards the back of the group, a young soldier with ginger hair the ruddy-faced look of a farmer's son – which he was – bore no malice but showed he knew where the younger man had been two afternoons before. Victor Hugo House, dubbed affectionately the *Liebnest*, was a whore house, where French women, brought over from Normandy, were regularly used by the rank and file German soldiers to ensure that their sexual frustrations were catered for, and that they didn't feel the urge to rape any of the island girls they saw daily in the streets.

Before the Americans had taken Normandy and marched onwards, towards the French port of St Malo, the girls were changed regularly to allow a new stock of peasant farm girls to ply their trade. Now, with this supply route cut off, the five women remaining had to service the German troops living in Jersey. It was not an enviable occupation.

'But what about Katrin, your wife?' asked Johan Wessel, a quieter, bookish man who had never come to terms with Nikki's womanising. There was a hush – no-one ever spoke about Nikki's wife unless he spoke about her first. Only the whisky could have induced the question or, indeed, an answer.

'It's my nature, Jan,' said Nikki, quietly. 'It's something I've always done – slept around. I make no pretence, and if Katrin wants to know, I'll tell her. Most of the time she doesn't ask. It doesn't mean that I love her less but it's my nature. Women were made for men to enjoy and if they invite me to enjoy them' – and he held his hands out, as if it were their fault, not his – 'who am I to refuse?'

'But what if Katrin sleeps with another man while you're away?' Wessel persisted, tentatively.

There was a pause, as the eight men looked at the one, curious to hear his reply.

'Then I'd kill her,' said Nikki, very quietly.

The momentary madness in his eyes and the silence was broken by moon-faced Thomas Schmidt changing the subject back to their reason for being there.

'But what I don't understand is the coal. Where does the bag of coal enter into our plan of attack? We steal into the bay. We sink three or four boats. We steal the coal barges and capture the hotel. But what for? To steal a bag of coal? Is the Kommandant so hard-pressed in his big granite house at the top of Mont Cochon that we have to steal a bag of coal for him?'

Laughter, and private Schumaker, who had been flicking through a copy of *Die Witsleining* interrupted. He looked owlishly over his wire-rimmed glasses and said, more to himself than to the others, listening: 'A body. A dead body it could be. Is that right, Nikki? Is the bag of coal a dead body we have to carry out?'

He, like all the others, trusted Jagmann and knew that if he could tell them the truth he would do so. He never lied to them and whenever possible let them know what lay ahead.

'It would be nice to think so,' said the Lieutenant. 'Winston Churchill, perhaps. He resembles most a sack of coal, in his black hat and black suit – about the same dumpy shape, too, but no . . .

'He's happy to stay in his bunker in England, just as our own dear Führer prefers to wage his battles from his bunker in Berlin. Perhaps the two should play war games in the same bunker, together, and let us go home . . .'

His attempt at deflecting the question was met with forced laughter from some of the others, but Schumaker persisted.

'But whose body?' he said. 'Whose body, Nikki?'

'A bag of coal.' Let us remember it as a bag of coal, for now . . .'

The Lieutenant, his glass empty, rose to his feet, pulled his jacket closed and yawned. It was time to go.

He smiled at the other men who were one by one struggling to their feet.

'A large, unwieldly bag of coal and very dirty.'

'Black and dirty like your women,' said Thomas, the Boy.

There was applause. They liked their leader; liked his relaxed style with them and knew that they could trust him to lead them well in battle. He was a man's man, and never thought of himself as any better than the men he led.

Just over six feet tall, with clear brown eyes and eyelashes that were almost too long – but not quite – Nikki was slim but muscular, with broad shoulders tapering to a narrow, almost womanly waist. He was lean and fit, with a grey fleck in his hair that some women found distinguished, attractive. He knew he had charm and animal magnetism like a contented cat; knew himself well enough to be able to draw the line between familiarity and contempt when dealing with his men, and knew that what he had said before about Katrin, his wife of five years who was currently living on the outskirts of Hamburg, in her parents' house, was true. If she slept with another man he wouldn't blame the other man – although he'd hate the comparison between them. He'd blame his wife without compunction and it would be she, not her lover, who would suffer the consequences.

8

A letter sent

'Dear Marte,' von Schellenberg began his letter. Then he stopped. It wasn't the sentiment he was afraid of, it was the fact that any letter he sent could become a death warrant for either of them, depending on the care with which he chose his words. So, consoling himself with the thought that even if he never sent the letter, at least it had been written, he began again:

My darling, darling Marte,

Be brave, my love, be brave, if not for your own salvation then for Eduard's and for mine, for without you my life will lose its meaning.

Every morning my first thought is of you; of your half-smile, the gentle way you would turn softly to me at night or the way you would reach up to me whenever I had my too-serious look on my face, to soften it with a kiss.

Here, in these beautiful, beautiful islands, the war touches us only occasionally, although we have seen the war in France and heard the explosions as our brave young men fight back against all the odds. Without the Americans the British would be nothing; just as without your love I, too, would be a defeated man.

You must trust our love, and cling to it, if not for

now, then for after the war, and have no doubts that we will see each other again. My uncle, who still has some say in the débacle of military command, knows of your plight and he has assured me, as much as anyone can do in these desperate times, that he will gain your release.

Marte, I know of your fears, both for your brother, and for me. My life is at least tolerable – if being forced to eat swede soup and limpets every day, to be washed down with herbal coffee, could be said to be 'tolerable'. And it amuses me to find that war has become a matter of filling in forms and dealing with petty squabbles from petty-minded islanders who we treat well, who eat better than we do, and yet who must insist on complaints of the most tedious kind, of stolen lettuce plants, of broken fences, or of their pets disappearing because they have food and our soldiers, having none, are desperate for meat . . .

They don't suffer the consequences of war as we do – as our young men who die in France do or as you do, my dear sweet thing, having become a prisoner in your own home . . .

There is a pointlessness to this island existence; waiting, always waiting, with no-one to share my love.

When this war is over, Marte, I will bring you back to this island to show you the sun and the beaches and my large granite house which, like the island, is as much my prison as your cell is yours.

Last night, Marte, as I began to undress for bed, for no reason it appeared to me that we all live inside our dreams and that infinity – something so huge and everlasting – begins wherever you want it to. Infinity begins at the end of my bedpost; and all I want to do is to reach across it and through it, just to touch you for one brief moment of time.

It's a nonsense, I know, but it gave me an odd sense of reassurance. Infinity can begin wherever you want it to. It can begin here, at the tip of my finger reaching out, touching you and then returning, the perfect circle, back to me in my cold granite room.

I explain it badly, of course, and rarely have I ever written a letter such as this. But I have to believe that there is a point to this war; and that you, and I, will see it through. So, my love, my Sperlingspapagel, here's to infinity; to my hard wooden bed, and to our unbreakable love. Stay alive, my own sweet princess; for both our sakes, stay alive; this war cannot go on forever, even if the little Austrian house-painter would like us to fight on until the end of time.

It was a letter von Schellenberg desperately wanted to send, but could do so only via Fr Otto Lossinger, a Roman Catholic priest he had known as a neighbour before the war in Bavaria, and had come to know and respect in recent months as a friend and father-confessor.

Like the old baron his father before him, von Schellenberg was a pragmatic Christian, a regular attender at Mass and occasional reader in church, but not so devout that he could ever put God before his Homeland and family. Lossinger knew this, but knew also of von Schellenberg's great humanity, and had been quite touched in recent weeks by how the Kommandant seemed to be genuinely worried about the future of the island people. It was as if he were already anticipating and planning for the end of the war, a war he had told Fr Lossinger he could not see Germany winning.

With only a few flights direct to Germany each month, and with nearly all the mail carefully scrutinised unless it was addressed directly to someone at military headquarters, only Fr

Lossinger's mail would remain unopened as he sent it to the church of St Paul's, in Lotz. From here his letter would, Lossinger had told him, be taken within the day to his family home; and from there, he was sure, it would find its way safely to his wife in Vilseck. No-one other than himself and Marte should ever know the letter's contents; which was just as well, for if it fell into enemy hands it would reveal the inner turmoil he was going through and his firmly held belief that Hitler would fail.

So although he entrusted the one letter to Lossinger, who gave a brief nod of understanding as he was called into the office, he had already written a shorter, much more formal letter, which he hoped could neither compromise himself nor his wife and which would be posted along with the rest of his mail. This, he knew, would be read at least twice by the censors in Berlin before it reached his home.

It could be argued that von Schellenberg's sentiments were false. It could be said that having given in to his body's desire a mere ten days ago, he should not tell the lie that he was still in love with his wife, who, though attractive, was thirty-six years old and had borne him two sons, the elder, Michael, the head-strong one, already missing, 'presumed dead', somewhere in Russia.

Yes, von Schellenberg may have felt uneasy that while he had been enjoying a young girl's body in his big double bed, his wife was languishing in a cell in Germany; but he was a realist; and accepted that as his body needed sex as a temporary release, it was his soul which cried out for a great deal more. He loved his wife. Each day that they were apart he missed her more.

9

Faces in the rain

'FACES in the rain, just faces in the rain,' the Boy thought to himself as the torchlight flashed across a rain-spattered window through which he could see faces of men keen to get in. Each had a job to do but, of all of them, his was the most dangerous job of all, a fact he knew and accepted with pride, as he glanced once more behind him and walked quickly up the stairs.

Thomas Schmidt was 23, looked 16, and could wire explosives in such a way that they would detonate with pin-point accuracy after, say, thirty seconds, five minutes or, as his brief was today, twelve minutes. It was only a practice run of course – practice for the real thing in Granville – but the explosives were real and he would quite happily have used them to blow the hotel to smithereens if he had been asked to do so. He enjoyed explosions; or rather he enjoyed the power that being able to destroy property and life on such a large scale gave him.

He also enjoyed the respect he received from other soldiers in the platoon, other soldiers older and tougher than he, but not, he believed, as brave. You had to be brave to want to play with this stuff, which had no friend and knew no favour. Its only purpose was destruction, and although he knew his subject well enough to blow up anything from a dead oak tree to a bridge or even a hotel, he never underestimated the danger that he carried with him.

'Faces in the rain, faces in the rain' kept going through his mind as he made his way upstairs in the dark. He knew the steps well by now and no longer had to fumble his way up, using the handrail as his guide. Eleven, twelve, thirteen steps to the top. The first floor and then left, along a long, narrow corridor, and then another. He placed the explosive beneath one of the main concrete supports and moved on. In Granville they would be primed to explode for real; tonight they would be safe, unless he made some terrible mistake. One down, two to go. He raced on again, up another flight of stairs. 'Faces in the rain, faces in the rain . . .' Another placed, as he moved gingerly along the corridor and then downstairs again at the far end, guiding himself by the light of a torch.

As he climbed down the stairs he could sense the other men in the building, checking rooms – each with a set task and a given time to complete it. Somewhere nearby someone sneezed – 'von Brauchitsch,' he told himself, his mind only half alert to what else might be happening in the vast black building.

'Do that in the real raid and you could end up dead,' he thought, reminding himself to tease the bulky soldier, two years older than he, to take a handkerchief with him when they attacked Granville for real.

Two charges placed. One below, one on the second floor and one to be placed in the kitchens when the men had gone.

The first explosion in the kitchen would trigger the second and then the third. His orders were to make certain that there was a maximum amount of chaos, noise and confusion as the men pulled back from the hotel. If all went according to plan, the hotel would have been cleared before the first detonation; after that it would be up to the French to douse the flames and perhaps collect the bodies.

The Boy moved out, backwards, to get away from the room, very conscious of the time it had taken. In the back of his mind he had been counting. One minute forty-eight seconds he guessed so far, another forty-two seconds before he would make his escape . . .

* * * *

THE explosion burst through the night air like a thunderbolt. It was the Boy who had let them down. The Boy, whose expertise everyone had respected; always so cool with explosives, always so confident as he played with his pieces of wire and putty. 'Damn him, damn him,' thought Hoffmeister as he watched flames leaping, soaring into the skies.

'Out. Get out. There may be another explosion at any moment.' Muhler, one of the soldiers closest to him, who had taken pride in being the third man in and one of the first out, turned as if to run back in.

'Don't be a damned fool,' said the Colonel. 'It's a hellhouse in there. Do you want to be blown up in hell?'

'But there are people in there – my friends,' said Muhler. 'Can't you hear them dying?'

It was true. Screams contrasted with the quietness of the night of a few minutes ago. Screams of pain, of terrible hurt, and the sound, too, of men thrashing about wildly, unable to escape. But Hoffmeister was not going to let anyone go back into that burning hell hole. He had only heard one explosion – a loud one from the second floor – but he knew there could be another two to come. Then the whole hotel, her support torn away, would fall inwards like a pack of cards. Anyone going back in would be crushed, not burnt to death.

After that first explosion there had been a rumbling sound as if a steam train was being driven through the corridors of the first floor of the hotel, and what appeared to be a tunnel of flames roared through, blowing out all the windows in a thunderball of fire. Some men dived out of the ground floor windows screaming. Another scream was cut short even before the man's blood boiled in his throat, while outside all was pandemonium, as several soldiers sought to approach the downstairs rooms but were beaten back by the heat of the flames, or were dissuaded from approaching by the cracking of walls and falling of chunks of hotel masonry.

'Get back!' snarled Hoffmeister. 'No-one goes in and that's an order!'

Relieved that the decision had been made for them, the soldiers outside, who had until then been enjoying their training runs to capture the hotel, watched, open-mouthed, as this spectacular free firework display puffed huge clouds of smoke and ash into the damp night air. They forgot the drizzling rain, forgot, too, that they were part of a hand-picked band of a hundred and eighty men selected for this raid on Granville, and held their breath, wondering if any more of their own could, by some crazy miracle, survive the flames.

Then first one man, and then another, appeared from the hotel, through a window furthest away from the kitchen where the first blast had been heard. A third man staggered into view through a doorway which belched out smoke and flame together, but this man was moving like a full-size puppet in a slow motion movie, as if drowning in the air. His face, in the glow of the fire, was melting away; his was a face distorted by pain and melting flesh. This was not a man; this was some grotesque beast come to haunt the soldiers watching outside.

The beast, moaning and crazed, fell to the ground as three soldiers ran towards him, only to recoil from the heat emanating from his burning body. They took off their jackets and threw them over the writhing, red-black thing in front of them which mouthed over and over again: 'Burning. I'm burning. God almighty, I'm burning,' but the sound was cracked and unreal.

'Get the medics,' Hoffmeister yelled at one of the three men who were all staring stupidly down at the smoking body of the dying man.

'You' – to another – 'phone the hospital. Tell them to clear out a ward ready for us.

'You,' to another man. 'Wake up von Schellenberg and tell him what's happened. Tell him it's an emergency. We need the best doctors, plasma, all the drugs – tell him everything. And the trucks. We need trucks to get these men to hospital.'

As the men started into action and as Wilhelm Hoffmeister busied the others, urging them to stop the fire from spreading, he looked up again at the building, his attention caught by a sizzling noise, followed by another dull boom and a terrific blast of heat.

This was the second explosion, proving that the Boy had done the job well. Every remaining window was blown out, showering the grass and nearly reaching his men standing well back, perhaps fifty yards away. With the main supporting walls and pillars buckled or broken, the hotel, as Thomas Schmidt had so accurately predicted, fell inwards, promising death for anyone trapped inside.

'Gott in Himmel,' swore Hoffmeister, as he realised what that odd smell was, drifting across the neatly cut lawn of the hotel. It was a sweet smell reminiscent of pork; but it was no ordinary meat and no ordinary fire. Some of his men were roasting in there and all he could do was to stand outside, watching their funeral pyre, powerless to save them.

He turned, and although sickened by the smell of roasting meat noted with approval that his lieutenants were already counting numbers, and checking men's names.

Dietrich was the man who had died in front of him on the lawn. He remembered the man vaguely, small and nervous, who had to hear a joke twice before he'd understand the punch-line. One dead. The Boy, Thomas Schmidt – two dead. Another, too close to the building to be approached and identified – three dead.

He wondered how many more there would be. 'How many out?' he asked Korporal Bruegel.

'Twenty-five, sir.'

'How many unaccounted for?'

'Twelve sir, with four seriously injured, two badly burnt, one with a head wound and another with a leg hanging off at the knee. Chopped through by falling glass as he was about to climb into the hotel, sir. Eischmann – the last man in.'

Two army trucks drew up, their headlights pitiful glimmers compared with the brightness of the burning hotel.

'As soon as we can be sure that the fire won't spread to the outhouses and the trees I want everyone out of this area.

Everyone. By morning I want no trace of us being here.'

'What about the men inside?'

There was a pause.

'Leave Jagmann in charge and four others. Those who are dead,' and his eyes rested briefly on the still smouldering corpse of Dietrich, 'have them examined by a doctor. No inquest. After the doctor comes and they have been identified, and the cause of death has been recorded, wake up an undertaker – a reliable one – and have them taken away and buried first thing tomorrow.

'You know what to do with their effects. But the sooner this mess is cleared up, the better.'

'The fire brigade, sir?'

Another pause. The flames were rising into the softly raining night and although they lit up the sky above the white skeleton of a hotel still blazing, they had not spread to the trees or the outhouses.

Hoffmeister knew that the blaze wouldn't go unnoticed or without comment from the islanders, and that even now prying neighbours would be daring to look outside to see what was happening. He also knew that they would not risk the wrath of the German army by appearing at the scene unless invited to do so.

'No fire brigade, Willie.'

This was not Hoffmeister's voice, but von Schellenberg's. As soon as he had heard of the fire he had come, and now he stood in the firelight, the moisture on his peaked cap reflecting the flames.

The informality of that first name. Only in extremes did he use his officers' first names, only in moments of deep elation or sorrow.

'We want no-one to know of our purpose here. Only those who need to know. And in the hospital you will tell the nurses and doctors that the explosives store caught fire. A careless match, a cigarette end – anything but the truth. Understand.'

And with a curt nod to both men, von Schellenberg walked

away from them, to the outskirts of the hotel, pausing only briefly to lift the sheet from the corpse which was being stretchered away from the grass.

'A small man, no taller than a boy,' von Schellenberg judged, looking at the charred face and the black, congealing blood. 'And he died in pain; terrible pain,' he said, quietly, as if to take consolation in the words, as he looked at the twisted mouth and the sightless eyes of a man who had volunteered to take part in the raid so that he could tell his mates back home that he, too, had done his fair share of fighting. Now he was twenty-one years old, a former carpenter, blond-haired, blue-eyed and dead.

As the body was loaded up into the back of the truck and as he watched another two men being helped to safety from the other side of the hotel, von Schellenberg, greatcoat collar up, hands together behind his back, stood on a small grass hillock and just looked. But his eyes, to anyone who dared look at them, were clouded over, unseeing.

His thoughts were of men caught in an unrehearsed, unwanted explosion, a cruel way to die brought about because one man had been either too casual or too clumsy. In the past few months he had found it increasingly difficult to maintain an appetite for war. Only a fool – or a Kreiser – could believe that Germany would win the confrontation. Besieged or swept back on every front, the German army, once the most-feared in the world, was being dismantled by the Allies in a merciless, methodical, inexorable way. And what for? To give succour to the ego of a Jew-hating madman, who would destroy himself and in so doing take his country with him.

Who knew how many other innocent pawns, like his wife, Marte, were being held and tortured in the Fatherland in the Führer's name? And these were patriots; people who loved their country, just as much as any front-line soldier.

Von Schellenberg looked again at the burning hotel and at the soldiers and medics as they scurried around in the cool of the night. As his eyes became used to the darkness, the shadows in the grass reached out further and further as he looked at them, shaping themselves into images not of dead soldiers but of his brother-in-law and wife, one almost certainly dead, killed for his part in the plot against Hitler, the other a woman he hadn't seen for eighteen months and might never see again.

Despite von Schellenberg's deepening resolve that the Granville raid must not be in vain, that they must capture the American general and use him to barter their way to the kind of peace their country could live with, he had no illusions about this latest set-back. With the explosion and deaths at the Emerald Hotel, von Schellenberg knew, with absolute certainty, that Vice-admiral Kreiser had the lever he had been waiting for to force him from office.

10

Ambition realised

'GOT him!' cried Kreiser. It was 4.30 in the morning and for the past five minutes he had been on the phone. As von Schellenberg's chief of staff he had had to be told about the disastrous exercise at the Emerald Hotel – although the General had deliberately not phoned until all the men had been accounted for, the corpses removed, the casualties taken to hospital and as much of the mess as possible cleared away.

The hotel was now a smouldering hulk, guarded by soldiers from the 619 Infantry Division, who had orders to arrest any islanders who decided to creep out into Bagatelle Lane to see what was happening. Later they would be relieved, and as soon as it was daylight a much more thorough clearing-up operation would begin. All the men who had been billeted there had been moved down into St Helier, to the Golden Apple Hotel, next to the Weighbridge where, on von Schellenberg's orders, Colonel Hoffmeister had told them that they were to tell no-one about what had happened.

Meanwhile, after spending two hours at the Emerald, where General von Schellenberg and Jagmann had worked busily, ordering sea water to be pumped around the outhouses and wooded area to prevent the fire from spreading, the Island Kommandant had travelled with the last of the wounded men to the hospital.

He had been told by Colonel Hoffmeister that seven people

had died in all – three outside on the grass and another four, thought to be trapped somewhere inside. Three others were badly burnt, one had been badly cut by falling glass and Klaus von Aufmann, 28 years old and with a wife and two children back home in Munich, was virtually unrecognisable as the cheerful city dweller who hadn't seen his family for the past two years.

As von Schellenberg leant over over him slightly, as he lay heavily sedated in bed, he realised, with a profound sense of self-loathing, that because of these preparations for the Granville raid Aufmann's children would never recognise their father again. It wasn't simply the face, one side so normal, the other incomplete, half-blown away; it was the other detail, like hands in huge bags, filled with liquid; hands looking like badly-made black gloves with the fingers cut away at the knuckle.

Von Aufmann had already faced one emergency operation by the time von Schellenberg arrived at the hospital and he knew that they would be operating again soon to try to repair at least some of his face and hands. He also knew that whatever magic healing powers the surgeons might possess, Klaus von Aufmann would, if he recovered, become just another war-torn cripple, living on hand-outs from the State . . . if the State ever managed to win this damned stupid war.

Before clicking his heels together and saluting the young Irish nurse who had treated this soldier so well and promptly, von Schellenberg said, in a subdued voice: 'Thank you for your help.' He followed that with a request that would have been the same in any language: 'Please keep him alive.'

The nurse replied: 'I'll try to do that, sir. He's a man like any other. We'll do our best.'

And then he left the ward to telephone Kreiser from the tiny office in the Gloucester Street hospital.

It was a short call, explaining exactly what had happened. And Kreiser, at the other end of the telephone, said little by return other than 'I see' and 'a tragedy'. There were no commiserations for those who had died nor concern about those still living. Kreiser; as efficient as ever, wanted to know what he should do according to the rulebook. Simultaneously he was thinking ahead about how best he could profit from this von Schellenberg-orchestrated tragedy. It was a tragedy for the soldier and his unfortunate men, but a sign from the gods that Ernst Kreiser was about to earn his rightful place in history. As he climbed back into bed the Vice-admiral was too excited, too conscious that the Fates had conspired to promote his star to fall into sleep again.

For that is what had happened: the Fates had taken a hand. For the next hour or so as he lay awake he played mind games about the wording of the telegram he would send from the islands to Germany. Even in this respect good fortune was on his side, for the only direct lines to Berlin were through the naval communications centre underground at St Jacques, on the outskirts of St Peter Port, in the other main island, Guernsey. The army might control the land, but – and the mere hint of a smile crossed Ernst Kreiser's face – the navy controlled the airwaves. Every time von Schellenberg wanted to contact Berlin, he could do so only with his permission. And because Vice-admiral Kreiser had direct access to the Führer he had already, on several occasions, taken the opportunity to explain his own views on the running of the islands, while complaining bitterly about how relaxed von Schellenberg had become in regard to discipline. The soldiers rarely saluted unless told to do so; they dressed shabbily; they had begun to listen to the island's inhabitants, who told them lies about who was winning the war. Now, with seven men killed and three badly injured in a practice run to capture a seaside town in northern France, they couldn't ignore his right to succeed the discredited army officer. Why, it would be almost too easy to leapfrog him – having made the right clucking noises in sympathy as he did so – he decided, with a happy smile on his face. He could almost pity his aristocratic adversary if he didn't dislike him so much, having good reason, he believed, to detest a man whose background, whose easy rise to the top of the military tree and whose easy use of command made him such a hero to his men. They were all qualities he had had to earn as he fought his way up the greasy pole towards power.

Perhaps with this disaster the men of 619 Division would finally turn against their Kommandant; perhaps they would realise that the time had come for a new military leader, someone who would lead them fearlessly and who wouldn't relinquish the islands without, as he saw it, using the British people who lived here as a shield, and using every man under his command to fight behind that shield, if necessary to the death.

11

Confession

18 AUGUST, 1944: Hotel Normandie was very quiet, just a few birds wheeling above, a child on the promenade, another on the seashore. An old woman out shrimping with her net was oblivious to the big black limousine in the hotel courtyard, to the sentries flanking the main lobby entrance, to the Stars and Stripes and Union Flag flying on either side above the door.

'St Malo has fallen, General. Just a few pockets of resistance. We've started mopping them up . . .'

Lieutenant Mike Muskie replaced the phone and drawled again: 'Won't take more than a day or two, I guess.'

At which General Dwight E Eisenhower, a burly man, with an easy charm it was difficult to dislike, even when he was tearing you off a strip, pushed back his chair and wandered towards the window. He noticed the old woman and enjoyed the tranquility of the beach, before his gaze was caught by a puff of smoke from the other side of the town. Almost certainly it came from the old French barracks, he realised, which were always damp and cold, come rain or shine. In America they would have been modernised or pulled down years before, but in France no-one seemed to bother. If they could be used they would be used. They were a left-over from Napoleonic days, he guessed, as he wondered how the French soldiers billeted there enjoyed being cooped up in a 19th century stone building with narrow windows and non-existent facilities. In the kitchens and the bathroom, on the hottest summer's day, water ran ice-cold to the touch. No-one liked being stationed there, and the French looked at the Americans, in their soft hotel beds with a mixture of jealousy and contempt. Eisenhower could understand their feelings – it wasn't fun walking barefooted over cold flagstones to wash in primitive conditions in a whitewashed room.

He knew the barracks and this area well by now. When was it? Six weeks ago he'd first set up camp. Arriving shortly after they'd taken Cherbourg, early in July, he organised a base here because it allowed him a moment of tranquility before they continued the push into Brittany. Tranquility. So unlike the savagery of D-Day and the terrible loss of life they'd had to endure fighting inland from the beaches.

Most of western France was now, in effect, his. There was the prospect of the final battle for Germany, the mopping-up of the war, but for a while at least he had time to himself, to catch up on all the paperwork and pen-pushing he'd deliberately ignored but which were necessary if they were to maintain the momentum and keep the supply lines open. More orders to be signed: this agreeing that coal could be imported, that agreeing that medical supplies could be unloaded. Without orders such as these the war effort would slow down or break down. France must become free again, but she would be set free only with the help of Allied administration.

Eisenhower wiped the back of his neck and looked out towards the sea. Now where were they – the islands? He'd heard there were 70,000 hungry people living somewhere out there, and was curious about how long they'd survive. Rumour had it that for meat they were killing and cooking domestic pets. How long before it would be rats or boiled-up leather? He looked away: it wasn't his concern.

He turned back to the lieutenant, who was busy typing out orders and counter-orders on a battered and very noisy portable machine.

'Time to pack up and move on, Mike,' he said, 'back to the

front line. Best go now before they say that all Ike Eisenhower's good for is a pension and a place by the sea.'

He chuckled at the half joke, before glancing again towards the old woman making her way slowly towards steps leading from the beach to the seawall. In a battered tin saucepan she was carrying enough shrimps for a seafood meal for one.

He ran his hand across his brow and turned back to the desk. Later on it would be hot – very hot – but a sea breeze, fresh with the morning, and the gentle rise and fall of the sea lapping against the shore made a nonsense of this war. Who could dream of fighting on a day such as this? The fisherwoman, realising that the American was looking at her from the hotel window, smiled, and waved.

Eisenhower would miss the humanity and warmth of the Granville people.

* * * *

6 March, 1945: General von Schellenberg crumpled up the telegram and wondered what would happen to him on his return to Germany.

He no longer had any illusions about his role in this war. And if this were demotion – or worse – his main concern was for Marte. What would happen to her? He felt more and more isolated, not least because he had few allies left in High Command, and the further he slipped, the less he could do for his wife.

He re-read the telegram. 'Due to ill-health Lieutenant-general Pieter von Schellenberg, commander of the 619th Infantry Division and Commander-in-chief of the Channel Islands is transferred to the supreme command of the Army's officers' pool. Vice-admiral Ernst Kreiser, Sea Defence Commandant and Chief of staff, Channel Islands, is appointed Commander-in-chief, with immediate effect. Lieutenant-general von Schellenberg is to return home at once, without awaiting the arrival of the new Divisional Commander.'

The telegram had been sent to the St Jacques bunker in Guernsey three days after the explosion at the Emerald Hotel before being forwarded to him here, but it said nothing about the Granville raid and gave no detail of von Schellenberg's supposed ill-health. 'Ill-health?' It was a lie – he hadn't been seriously ill in years! Why, even that morning he'd taken his customary dip in the sea – ten minutes he allowed himself – and before that he had enjoyed a horse ride across the beach.

But at least Kreiser could wait. He had a whole day before the next plane was due to land; at least twenty-four hours before he would hand control over to his rival.

Von Schellenberg continued to write in a neat, sloping hand. Exercise and writing – the one for his body, the other for his mind – had both been activities he'd enjoyed during his stay. He had even written a book about the islands for his troops, telling them of their attractions and using photographs he had taken of some of the beaches and bays. It might have been vanity to write the book himself, instead of delegating the task to one of his staff, but it had given him a keen sense of pleasure to send the first copy home, to his wife, and to Eduard, his youngest son, 13 years old and destined to become the next Baron von Schellenberg.

As well as writing 'Besetzung der Kanalinseln' since he had become Befehlshaber two and a half years ago, he had begun to keep a diary, although since July, 1944, and the bungled attempt to assassinate Hitler at Rastenburg, he had preferred to confide his thoughts not to paper but to an old acquaintance from before the war, the Catholic priest Fr Otto Lossinger, the only German minister to the troops in the islands. It was to the likeable, grey-haired cleric, whose shambling gait and untidy appearance were a parody of an absent-minded professor, that the Island Kommandant had first confided his belief that Germany could not win the war, and it was Otto Lossinger who had helped to smuggle the last letter he'd written home to his wife. In effect, Fr Lossinger had become his listening diary, and before he left on tomorrow's flight to Berlin he must make a point of seeing him for the last time – to see if he had heard any news about his wife and to thank him for his support during the past nine months.

The phone rang. This was to be the briefing; the final briefing. It was to be his last day in charge but first he must talk with his friend, Colonel Hoffmeister.

He scratched the side of his nose with the pen and looked again at the list in front of him. He was writing reports to wives and mothers, telling them that their husbands or sons had died in action. Notification of death was brief, formal. 'It is with deep regret . . .' No mention of the smell of flesh burning or the glazed-eyed look of a dead man's body.

'You sent for me, Herr Kommandant.'

Hoffmeister was unusually formal today – did he know what had happened to his friend? But after the most precise salute, the most deafening clicking of heels and the stiffest of bows, Hoffmeister relaxed and was once again the bluff soldier von Schellenberg knew so well.

'I was seeing if I could remember what it is to give an officer a correct salute,' he explained. 'Not bad, even if I say so myself,' he added, looking down at von Schellenberg and realising that something was preying on his mind.

Von Schellenberg smiled back, wearily. He knew that Hoffmeister might never make general but would always be a man to be feared and respected by men both above and below him.

'The Granville raid,' said von Schellenberg.

'Yes, Herr Kommandant.'

'It will go ahead as planned two nights from now.'

A pause, then: 'Yes, Herr Kommandant.'

'When it does go ahead I will not be here, or in any way involved.'

Silence, then: 'No, Herr Kommandant.'

'Because of ill-health I am returning to Germany.'

'Ill health?' A puzzled stare. 'But you're never ill, sir. Is it something the doctors . . ?'

'No,' said von Schellenberg, with an attempt at a smile. 'I am beginning to wonder if it is my ill-health or the ill-health of others, many hundreds of miles away. But I cannot leave until a plane is sent for me and that will not be until at least tomorrow. Until then I remain in charge. I do not go until tomorrow and my command will not end until tonight. After that you will report directly to Kreiser. Do you understand, Willie?'

Hoffmeister knew, or rather could guess what had happened all right. Everyone knew there was no love lost between the two men, although no-one was quite sure why. Some thought it might have been that von Schellenberg was army, Kreiser navy, but even this didn't explain the almost visible loathing they appeared to have for each other.

And for Hoffmeister? To lose von Schellenberg now, because of poor health? It was mad, a crazy insult to his friend.

'Even if you are ill,' said Hoffmeister, trying to choose his words carefully. 'Even if you are ill, surely you would not wish to leave the Island until the raid has been carried through. Surely High Command would not wish this to be so.

'And if you *are* ill – wouldn't it be best for you to stay here, to convalesce? Surely life in Germany can't be that much better and healthier for you than if you were to stay here?'

He was trying, in the most delicate of ways, to advise his friend to stay, to bluff his way through in the hope that the situation would improve.

'I had thought of that,' said von Schellenberg, allowing a brief smile to touch his face, 'but I must be seen to leave the place of my own free will and to climb on board the plane unaided. I am no hero, but I have some pride. Remember, though, that the key to this operation's success lies with you. You have trained the men. You know their strengths and weaknesses. And when I am gone nothing – nothing – should prevent the raid from going ahead.

'Two nights ago was a one in a million accident. We don't know what the Boy did wrong but until then all the practice raids had been going remarkably smoothly. The raid must go ahead and your priority must be to capture the General. With

Vice-admiral Kreiser in charge your duty must still be to bring him here, and recognise his value. You – I charge you, old friend, with the task of the General's safe capture.'

'But what if he does something stupid, or something goes wrong?'

It was a fair question to ask, not least because Hoffmeister was worried about his future under the control of another man, and a naval man at that.

Von Schellenberg's last words, before the two friends walked together to the main hall for the final briefing, were riddled with bitterness.

'Nothing will go wrong. But if it does, give Kreiser what he wants, give him his war. With Eisenhower dead all eyes would turn towards our island fortress. The Americans would demand revenge; the British would feel it their duty to recapture their islands and Kreiser would be able to mount a rearguard action, defending the islands until every man, woman and child had been forced to suffer. If you cannot capture the General, kill him. Kill him, and let Kreiser suffer the consequences and become a martyr.'

12

A woman's man

NIKKI Jagmann was a womaniser. He admitted it freely to his men. They, in turn, felt a combination of respect for him as a man, but they also spared more than a little sympathy for his wife Katrin, especially those who had met the vivacious young woman, who adored her husband for all the wrong reasons. For the past eight years she had put up with her husband's amatory misdeeds, only once asking for the truth after he had pursued – and won – one of her own close friends. The truth which was revealed could have killed her love for him but he had insisted the affair had meant nothing and that although he might be tempted again, it would never be with the delightful Elsa. Her legs were too fat, and although she dressed smartly she had done little exercise to regain her figure since the birth of her son.

After that Katrin never asked about his suspected infidelities, and although she remained on speaking terms with Elsa, thenceforward she saw her, and her other, prettier friends less frequently and in a new light. She continued to love Nikki, and took him gladly to her bed, but nowadays she looked forward to his becoming an older man. Perhaps his capacity for loving – or rather sexing, for he had sworn his love to her on the Bible – others as well as herself would fade and die as he became wiser. This was her only consolation, but it ignored one very basic fact – Nikki. His father had been the same until, at the age of sixty-five and no longer able to attract a pretty woman, every once in a while he would treat himself by paying for one. Like father, like son. Without doubt, as Nikki grew older if he couldn't attract a woman by his looks and personality he would do so with his money.

To Nikki any woman was fair game – 'if it moves, den Hof machen' had been his crude, but often-repeated philosophy. But that said, he also liked class, and nearly every day when he walked from the officer's house at Five Oaks, taking the Mont Millais road to Victoria College where military headquarters had been established four years before, he would see it.

He began his walk at eight, arriving at 8.15 am exactly, and most days when he walked he would pass the same mother and daughters walking the other way. Two daughters, one about nine, the other about six or seven. They and their dark-haired mother were all attractive, with an attraction that was more than just physical good looks. The mother oozed class. Not so much money, more good taste in clothes, manners . . . and daughters.

For just over five months they had passed each other almost daily, each on the other side of the road. He would smile. They would ignore his smile, and quicken their pace. Which meant that for five and a half months they had been respectful enemies. Her husband, Nikki knew, was a British officer who had left several months before the German Occupation.

'Over four years without a man. 'What a waste,' thought Nikki, who couldn't bear to see a good-looking woman not being regularly serviced. Although he occasionally missed his wife and, even more so, his two charming children back home in Düsseldorf, they had always been a separate part of his identity. From the age of 14 he had accepted without qualms that where women were concerned availability was more important than looks – but looks and availability were most rewarding of all.

In some ways, to a man of Nikki's character, the war had come at just the right time in his life. Bored with small town morality, he had eagerly seized the chance to join Hitler's new army when it annexed the Saarland in 1935. He had been older when he had volunteered than many of the other men – he was twenty-two, and it was four years before the war proper began – but he had no regrets. An army life had given him the opportunity to see other places, other excitements, other girls, many of whom, in such violent times, gave in more readily than if this had been a sedentary, normal world of nine to five office hours.

Nikki was thirty-one now. A hardened soldier, he had been there when Austria was finally taken and had seen his stay in the Channel Islands as a temporary measure, a stepping stone to London and the pretty English women he had heard so much about.

So, although he was naturally happy to be alive and well and living in Jersey, where occasional affairs with Irish, French and local girls made it much more fun to be living here than fighting on the Russian front, he craved activity. He needed the adrenaline to be pumping through his veins before he went into military action; the quick reactions needed to train a gun on a man before deciding whether to pull the trigger; the nerveless ease of command and bonhomie with his men who, in an asexual way, he could love much more easily than any of his conquests.

This English woman had been different, however.

Three weeks before it had begun. The woman and her children had been returning to their home with a hefty load of logs they had been given, perhaps by a friend. There were too many logs and they were too awkward to carry up the hill without a struggle, and so at first protestingly, and then gratefully, the woman had allowed Nikki to carry her burden to her home in Palace Close.

It had made Nikki an extra twenty minutes late – but it had been worth it.

She had thanked him – coldly, which he expected, despite the ready smile – hadn't, of course, invited him in, but had at least offered a ghost of a smile at Nikki's laboured attempt at English conversation.

His help that day also meant that Nikki knew where she lived. The next day he hadn't seen her. But the morning after that she was there again, this time walking, as usual, with her pet

Sealyham terrier and the girls. This time she had returned Nikki's cheerful 'good morning' with a 'good morning' of her own.

Chat, a sense of humour, and an obvious appreciation for what he wanted to conquer were all important weapons in Nikki's cheerful disarming of women. He knew his English was bad, but the badness could be subtly deliberate, for it allowed him to use this apparent inability to communicate to good effect. He had discovered this many times before. The secret was to fill the silences with a search for words. The words turned to actions and the actions and his own beguiling nature did the rest, leading, on occasions, to nights of pleasure with some lovesick woman who for too long had shared a bed with no-one but her own desperate imagination.

The Sunday after that first meeting Nikki had made a point of collecting a large bundle of firewood from a hillside in the west of the island, near the airport, and out of bounds to civilians. He had loaded it into the back of his vehicle and had driven back into town, to leave it on Mrs Bradwell's doorstep. Mrs Michelle Bradwell: twenty-seven years old, with two daughters, Kate and Emma, he had discovered, by looking in the files of all the English women left in the island.

When he called that day he had left no message, just the bundle of wood. But the next day, the Monday morning, he had asked her, from across the road, whether she had been pleased with her extra little present.

'Yes. Thank you. I didn't realise the wood had been left by you. Thank you very much.'

It was all clipped tones and severity, but he sensed – no, he knew – that this was something of an act. The ice was breaking. She would have walked on, but having broken her defences down like the hunter he was, he pressed his advantage home.

'Is there anything else you want?' he asked, conscious of his heavy German accent.

'No. Nothing thank you. Only . . .'

The 'only', he realised, was a second thought, as if there were something troubling her, at the back of her mind.

He pressed forward, taking the initiative.

'Only what?' he asked.

'Only – I don't suppose you have any chocolate, do you?' The woman's voice was a combination of eagerness and caution, the eagerness taking over as she said the words and they tripped over themselves in a desire to be heard. 'Only . . . I had promised the girls that one day they would taste a piece of chocolate – they've never had any to try and I, and I . . . But no,' she said, quickly, having seen a passer-by cast a quizzical look at this woman so obviously engaged in conversation with a German.

'No, nothing, don't, I . . .' And she blushed, apologetically, and walked on.

Firewood and chocolate. The game was continuing, and Nikki, well-versed in the gambits of sexual psychology, wondered if these were the only gifts he would have to make before enjoying her in bed.

* * * *

THE chocolate bar had cost him ten Reichmarks and a little bullying before he had bought it from one of the black market traders in town. And this time, he thought, as he strolled towards Mrs Bradwell's large, out-of-town house, in its own large, out-of-town garden, he would visit her indoors and not outside in the streets.

It was Monday, 12th February, he recalled, when she had first invited him in. Casually dressed, he had knocked on the door well aware that if the neighbours had seen him in his grey German uniform, with the Iron Cross, first class, on the jacket, he would have been deliberately snubbed, for in an area such as this any man in a German uniform could only mean one thing – the enemy. Similarly, he well knew that if he hadn't been carrying the gift, there would have been no reason to expect anything more than a brief conversation and a door closed in his face.

It was a calculated risk he was taking, like a fisherman, wondering if, after all his preparation, the fish would bite. But his bait was taken – albeit reluctantly. The fish bit – reluctantly, it must be admitted – and despite his disarming smile he realised she had reservations; but once she was hooked all he had to do was to play the line, and be his normal, naturally charming self. In good time he would reel her in . . . a good catch, well worth having. And afterwards? Well, why not let nature take its course?

After a tentative few minutes, hovering on the doorstep, Mrs Bradwell had little alternative but to invite Nikki in. The chocolate bars had proved extremely good bait. After she had led him through to the kitchen, not really knowing how far to repay his kindness, she had asked him to sit down, made him a painfully thin cup of black coffee, and tolerated his presence.

The two girls had stayed in the kitchen while they talked, both of them obviously fascinated, for neither had spoken directly to a German before.

'What is your name?' he had asked of the little one, the six-year-old.

Suddenly shy, little Kate pretended not to hear, keeping the width of the table between them as their mother busied herself with the kettle.

'She's Katie. She's six,' said the elder one, daring not only to speak, but also to be rude to this interloper into their tidy lives. 'She's shy. We don't talk to Germans.'

There was a pause as Mrs Bradwell placed a coffee cup in front of her guest, her arm reaching across his face, left to right, to do so. As she went round to the other side of the table to be nearest her child Nikki couldn't help a small, inward smile.

She was wearing perfume. Despite the harshness of war, and no men to impress, she maintained the niceties of appearances. He liked that in a woman.

He cupped the fragile china cup in his hands and blew across the coffee, gently, to make it cool.

Mrs Bradwell noticed his neat, strong, long-fingered hands. There were no callouses, or the broken nails you would expect from a run-of-the-mill soldier. The hands gave her a confidence to talk to him. She could not possibly imagine such hands being used to ill-treat a man.

Nikki noticed the change of expression, and also realised that to get to the woman he would first have to gain confidence in the children.

'You like the chocolate?' he said, as Mrs Bradwell gave each a square to sample.

'My Daddy's going to come home soon and kill you all,' said Katie, leaning her elbows on the table and munching, thoughtfully, the edges of her lips already speckled with chocolate.

'Don't take any notice of my Katie. She's only six and she doesn't really understand,' said Michelle Bradwell, alarmed by her daughter's unsolicited outburst.

'Have you got a gun?' asked Emma, cutting through her mother's red-faced apology and not at all interested in the frightened look in her eyes.

'Yes,' said Nikki, 'although I don't carry it around with me every day, and only occasionally fire it at people. Even then, I nearly always miss.'

He looked at the child's mother, trying to reassure her with his eyes.

'Why? Would you like to own one?' he said.

'No,' said Emma, alarmed at the thought. 'But I wouldn't mind seeing one work. Daddy showed me his once. It had six bullets in it. Real bullets,' she added, darkly.

'Now that's enough girls,' said Mrs Bradwell, afraid that every word her children spoke could cause her even more hardship than the hardship she currently had to bear. Two children, very little money, no man to look after her and no real friends in the island she and her husband had moved to seven years before.

'Don't worry,' said Nikki, with an open smile and a flash of white, even teeth in a brown-tanned face.

He was aware that she was slowly thawing; that her attitude towards him was changing. At first he had been a representative of the German Army. Now she was beginning to judge him for himself. He was heading into easier waters.

'Don't worry. I have my own children too, back home in

Düsseldorf. Children are the same everywhere. So – open? Is that the word I should like to use?'

Sensing that a confidence had been shared, Mrs Bradwell gave the apology of a smile by return and tried to shuttle the children out of the room. But they, intrigued by this man their father would return to the island to kill, were far more at ease in his presence than their mother.

'Have you ever *killed* anyone?' asked Emma, as she dared herself to walk towards him and as he lounged back a little in his chair. He even smelt foreign she decided, as she looked at his high German boots, black leather and neatly-shaped around his muscled calves.

Nikki's eyes tightened imperceptibly. 'Why should I kill somebody?' he asked. 'Is there someone here who you do not like?' This deflected the conversation neatly enough away from a downright lie. He looked up and directly into the eyes of Mrs Bradwell, across the other side of table. 'You must be lonely in this big house. Alone. Lonely,' said Nikki, as if trying to make up his mind which word was the most appropriate. 'Is there anything you need. Perhaps blankets, perhaps a little meat, or fish.'

The one-word answer, 'no', was spoken with some hesitation, as if the woman he had been looking at so intently would have preferred to make a very different reply. But he understood and perhaps admired her more for standing by her principles, even though it had probably been some months since her family had last enjoyed a proper meal.

Nikki, who had accomplished all he needed from this first visit, knew that the best time to leave was when first the icy barriers broke down.

'I will go now,' he said, standing up, and ruffling Katie's hair. Katie promptly went to a drawer, pulled a large pink comb out and unruffled it, ensuring as she did so that she was winning his attention.

The dog, which for most of Nikki's visit had been asleep in his basket near the back kitchen door shook himself, yawned and then lolled towards Nikki, as if welcoming an old friend. He patted the dog absent-mindedly.

'Meat,' he said. 'I will see what I can do.'

He straightened up and made towards the door. As he walked past the dog, and around the table, he made a point of passing as close as he could to Mrs Bradwell, who was now standing and moved slightly forward, obviously expecting him to go out of the front door, the way he had come in.

'I will not upset the neighbours,' he said, his eyes all the time on this most, most attractive of women as, almost by accident, his fingers ran no more than two or three inches along her spine as she tried to move the clumsy chair out of her way.

Nikki knew that she had been trying to keep this horrid German at least an arm's length at bay. But she had failed. He also knew that when his fingers touched her back she had responded. Involuntarily, it may have been, but it was enough.

He didn't look at her as he strode out, across the threshold. 'I will go but if I do find, by chance, a little meat, I will bring a little meat to you here, ja?'

'No, you mustn't.' And more than anything, more than anything in the world as he moved past her, to the door, Michelle Bradwell wanted this man to get out of her house and out of her life forever.

'Very well,' he said, turning, slightly, and shrugging his shoulders. Let her have doubts now. He knew he would return; she didn't. And he also knew, although she would never admit it, that underneath the hatred of his race, a hatred bred by war, not choice, she wanted him to return.

The business-like tone returned as he said a curt 'goodbye', bowed slightly and without either Nazi salute or clipping of heels walked quickly away to the back garden gate. He didn't look back.

Mrs Bradwell closed the kitchen door, gently.

'Will that man come back again, Mummy?' Katie said. 'Is he a Hun? A Nazi?'

'I don't know,' said her mother, half to herself. 'I don't know, Katie dear.'

13

Final briefing

VICTORIA College, 11 am, 6 March. Only the island's top public boy's school would have the audacity to dominate the north hill so completely, which it did, its granite façade resolutely looking down on the small red-brick houses below. Built nearly a hundred years before, at the height of the Gothic revival, the architect hadn't been content to make it either welcoming or functional. Spurning both, he preferred huge arches and the occasional high tower, incorporating buttresses and gargoyles. To any casual observer – although its domination was such that no one could 'casually' glance at it without feeling immediately intimidated – its cold beauty contained a church-like quality of religiosity, and if they had been invited inside, through the cloisters to the main school hall, that cathedral atmosphere would have dogged them every inch of the way. In part it must have been deliberate, to combine Christian awe and British learning, and several generations of schoolboy had grown up, never quite being able to untangle the concept of God from Mr Nevin, their headmaster. Because God, they knew, was an Englishman, the muddle didn't pose too many problems, so for almost a century Old Victorians had travelled the world, many of them in army uniform as they'd spread the Word to the Empire. And, because God was an Englishman, they thought nothing of dying for the sake of King and Country, which they had done particularly well during the Great War of 1914-18, when a hundred and twenty-five old boys had died fighting, many of them as officers on the Western Front.

Those doughty warriors would have been among the first to protest that here, in the cradle of their learning, in the main hall where they had sung so lustily the first few lines of 'Jerusalem', could be found the very enemy they had given their lives to destroy. There were nearly twenty of them in all, including a last-minute replacement for Thomas Schmidt, the older, more sedentary Joseph Beck. Willie Hoffmeister of course was here, but so too were Lieutenants Jagmann and Kesselring and Seekapitan Lindenheim, joined by another seaman who was to play an important part in the raid, Kapitanleutnant Heinrich Keiffer. They, and the other members of the group who would lead or play key roles in the raid were seated towards the front of the hall. Meanwhile, at the back, listening, but not speaking, his wooden schoolchair a respectful distance from the rest of the assembly, Vice-admiral Ernst Kreiser was content to listen to the Kommandant's final briefing. He saw no need to comment and, indeed, for much of the time seemed more interested in the architecture of the hall than the speaker: but this was not because he was against the raid – far from it. It was because he had his own ideas about the attack on Granville, and he knew he had the power to implement them with or without von Schellenberg's approval.

As he sat back in his chair, delighting in any discomfort his presence might cause to his rival, Kreiser's disinterest didn't go unnoticed by von Schellenberg, who had never wanted the Vice-admiral as his Chief of Staff, but had been given no alternative after the abortive army-led plot to assassinate Hitler at Rastenburg the previous July. That decision had been made in Berlin and passed on to Admiral Hassell, of Marinegruppe West, which nominally controlled the Channel Islands; nominally, because even as the decision was taken the Germans were pulling back, out of western France.

Kreiser's appointment was entirely political, based on the Führer's belief that no army officer was entirely trustworthy and that only the navy had remained loyal to him over the past two years. So even though there were fewer than seven hundred seamen but over twenty-five thousand soldiers in the islands, it was Kreiser whom the Führer and Hassell trusted: it was Kreiser they would listen to; and it was Kreiser, ambitious and unscrupulous, who was already plotting the downfall of his rival in power. Although supposedly the junior officer, his star was in the ascendancy while that of his rival in power was about to fall. Outwardly he remained calm at the meeting – bored, even. Inwardly he was seething with excitement. It wouldn't be long now before his dreams were realised; it wouldn't be long now . . .

At the front of the hall von Schellenberg looked no different than he had before the disastrous dummy-run to capture the Emerald Hotel. Whatever he was feeling inside didn't show to his audience, who were keenly aware that within the next seventy-two hours they would be at war in France. But even as he began to speak the General knew that deep within each man would be a question mark after the deaths of their friends in the explosion. He also knew that one of the best ways of regaining their confidence was simply to repeat what they had to do, and how they had to do it, as if nothing had changed.

Repetition. Drill, organisation and repetition – so boring but so vital at a time like this. If you lost confidence in your officers you could still take confidence from the plan. Time and time again they had gone over the details of the raid, time and time again they had hunched over the scale model of the French seaside town, having learnt the timetable of tides that week by heart.

This time, like Mr Nevin before him, von Schellenberg played schoolteacher, but he didn't see the need to hide behind a lectern, and the only prop he had was a large map, unrolled and pinned to a portable blackboard a little to one side of his desk. After a dry half-smile, directed to no-one in particular, he stood up, and began.

'As you know, there have been various practices at sea and on land. The last practice ended in disaster – but we persevere.

You have already studied photographs and a model of the town, its beaches, its fortifications, the tugs in harbour, the coal ships. By now you should know the town as if you had lived there all your life.

'The main body of the task force will rendezvous at 01.00 hours on Friday, 9 March, 1,000 metres offshore to the east of Granville. Even as you are preparing to strike against the enemy, three artillery carriers, the AF101, AF168 and AF171, under the captaincy of Heinrich Keiffer, will be attempting to draw off and engage the Granville guardship and any possible Allied air support.

'Captain Keiffer will lead the enemy south, towards the island of Grand Chausey, where he will destroy the Chausey lighthouse to make enemy pursuit more difficult in the blackness of the night. Afterwards they will make their way home.

'This will be their job: to guarantee you a safe passage to Granville, and back again. How well they do that job will be known to you only if your attempt to land in the harbour or your return to Jersey is hindered by air or sea attack.'

All eyes turned to Heinrich Keiffer, who could, it appeared, turn all their good work onshore to disaster off it. He met their looks with coolness. He was confident in his own ability; his self-assured smile and curt nod of the head were indications to his German colleagues that they had nothing to worry about.

Von Schellenberg continued.

'Captain Keiffer will have set sail for Chausey before the task force assembles. When it does, Colonel Hoffmeister, in the leading boat, will give the order to Lieutenants Kesselring and Jagmann to lower four boats which will ferry a large part of the task force to the north beach – here.'

He pointed to the northern beach on the map.

'The main assault detachment will have twenty minutes to land and to make their way into the heart of the old town.

'As soon as Colonel Hoffmeister is confident that the assault force is comfortably on its way to shore he will order three of the five ships under his command, the M62, M57 and auxiliary minesweeper M343 into the harbour. Meanwhile, the cutter FL17 and M160 will stand offshore to provide covering fire if necessary and to support the destruction of the lighthouse and radar station at the most westerly point of the old town, here, at Le Roc.

'By the time that Captain Lindenheim has manoeuvred the lead boat, the M62, past the harbour walls, the first assault force should be well on their way to taking complete control of the old town.

'The first detachment, under Lieutenant Jagmann, will already have taken the Normandie Hotel. For the next hour it will be under our control. As well as searching for documents and maps which will give High Command a clue to the Anglo-American intentions you will take prisoner any high ranking officers staying in the hotel. In particular you will look for one very important general.'

He paused, knowing from the way that the men were looking at each other that this merely confirmed what most of them had already guessed: that there was an added dimension to this raid on the small French town. But what they wouldn't know, with the exception of the five men he had taken into his confidence in February, was how important a hostage that American general might be.

The glances and shuffling ceased. Von Schellenberg continued.

'When the raid is coming to an end, and after Lieutenant Jagmann has guided his "guests" to the ships, the Hotel Normandie will be primed to explode within minutes.'

At the mention of the word 'explode' there was a slight burr of unease as everyone remembered what had happened to the last explosives expert. A few eyes also turned in the direction of an older, grey-haired man sitting slightly to one side, Joseph Beck, who was unused to such attention and who blushed redly at his fellow officers' sudden interest.

'As some of you are aware, Joseph Beck is taking over the responsibility for mining the hotel. By the time Beck has set the explosives the other two groups, the first under von Bastion, the second under Kesselring, will have returned to the boats, having led their raiding parties to the heart of the old town, where Lieutenant Kesselring's job will be to take over control of the Hotel des Ormes. This, we believe, is where several other American officers and their men will be stationed, most if not all of them fast asleep, believing they are many miles away from their intended enemy, the "intended enemy"' – and here von Schellenberg permitted himself the luxury of a wry smile – 'being us.

'Within the first twelve minutes of entering the hotel it must be ours. I want' – and the General's voice became a good deal harder – 'I want you to ensure that no-one living in the hotel will take any further part in this brief battle of ours.

'And, because the Hotel des Ormes lies less than a hundred yards from the new town, and is less than three minutes from the Hotel Normandie, five of Kesselring's men will mine the road and prepare for a possible ambush – here. On the boulevard Amiroux.' The General pointed at the neck of the land which joined the old, high town, with the new. The boulevard was the only road linking the two.

'Lieutenant von Bastion, meanwhile, will have led his troops through the town to the French barracks – here, above the harbour. With a handful of men we believe we can persuade the French to stay indoors. Of course they may decide to come out and make a fight of it, but we all know about the legendary fighting prowess of the famed French army.'

There was an appreciative round of laughter at von Schellenberg's heavy sarcasm. As someone who had fought against the 'famed French army' in two world wars it was obvious that he saw their presence in the harbour town as a matter of no great importance.

'. . . And with a few soldiers more he will destroy the radar station – here – as soon as possible.

'By the time von Bastion and Kesselring are well inside the town, the harbour will already be feeling the full impact of our German guns and it will be to the harbour that the members of each of the assault squads will return once their jobs are over. There they will be ferried back to the three minesweepeers, which will have been busy themselves for nearly an hour.

'At just after 01.30 hours Colonel Hoffmeister will have launched his own attack on the harbour installations, having first fired across the harbour, to do as much damage as possible and to keep the townspeople comfortably indoors.

'As the port burns, Colonel Hoffmeister and Captain Lindenheim will seize every coal-carrying vessel lying in harbour. Those that cannot be sailed back to Jersey will be destroyed. If the Colonel decides to go ashore to escort the American general back to his ship, Captain Lindenheim will remain in charge of all operations at sea. Although there may be some return of fire when we strafe the town and harbour, we do not believe that our enemy have any heavy artillery. If they want to make a fight of it, they will surely lose.'

Von Schellenberg's words revealed the true confidence he had in this attack: for he had spent many, many hours planning it and assessing the strength of the Anglo-American forces stationed there. If the guardship could be drawn away from the harbour the only artillery piece that La Haut Ville could muster was a 57mm gun and, if the Americans were to use this, first they must repel and defeat the German commandos as they stormed the two French hotels.

As von Schellenberg explained: 'If the first part of the raid is successful, if the Hotel Normandie falls, and if everyone is in the right place at the right time, make no mistake – once we enter the harbour, we have the upper hand. Very much so. By 02.50 hours, at the very latest, the raid will be over. We will be on our way home and you, gentlemen, will all be heroes.'

Von Schellenberg's Boys' Own enthusiasm for the Granville raid was apparent to all those listening; and they listened well and now in silence, licking their lips at the prospect of action at last. Action, their General was promising them, action in which they would have the upper hand in enemy territory.

'For one hour and fifty minutes, no more, I expect the old

town to be completely under our control. When the charges go off in the Hotel Normandie, you will already be on your way back to the boats – and we know from bitter experience the chaos that will ensue once those charges are blown.

'Gentlemen, you have studied the maps, the hotel, the defences. At last you will be making your own unique contribution to the war. Any questions?'

Kreiser replied, from the back. 'Herr Kommandant.' His voice was patronising, almost an insult. 'You say that all will go smoothly. Are you sure your explosives experts – on the quayside and in the hotel – are qualified to do this job? And have the men themselves enough confidence, after such a terrible disaster at the Emerald Hotel?'

He laid heavy stress on the word 'terrible', looking directly at von Schellenberg as he spoke. Everyone else in the room was quiet, sensing, like some tangible, physical thing, the hostility between the two men.

In reply the General's voice was low, but firm. 'We will never know how the explosion was caused, Vice-admiral Kreiser,' he said, 'but this I guarantee. Not only will the raid be successful, but the damage done to British and American pride will be inestimable. When the raid goes ahead – as go ahead it must – there will be no mistakes. Every officer here has assured me that he has confidence in his men, and I have no doubt that Oberleutnant Beck will allow no room for mistakes. He knows his trade: I have confidence in his professionalism and unless one of my officers wishes to question his ability to blow up the hotel, as we have practised, I see no reason to change my plan of action. But I will put it to the men.' His blue eyes slowly scanned the room. 'If any of you do not wish the raid to go ahead as it has been planned, speak now.' His voice softened. 'I will not hold it against you. But if you have doubts, do not wait until after the raid to tell me.'

No-one spoke; and although they all looked uncomfortable, particularly Beck, who was gazing down at the flagstone floor, unwilling to be a pawn in this confrontation between seaman and soldier, any doubts they may have had had took second place to their thirst for adventure.

'Nothing will go wrong, Herr Kreiser. Nothing.' Von Schellenberg's voice rose, but was as firm as a rock. His resolve was evident for all to see and hear. 'And the attack will go ahead, with or without my being here when the raiders return.'

This was the first official hint of his leaving, despite a rumour that he was being recalled to Berlin; some said to promotion in the beleaguered capital, others said to his arrest and trial for alleged treason. As far as von Schellenberg was concerned, however, only he and Hoffmeister knew the truth; and it came as something of a shock as he finished his speech that he could see no surprise on Kreiser's face at the hint that he would not be there when the task force returned. 'The son of a bitch knows,' he said to himself. 'The son of a bitch knows.'

Aloud, and without showing the discomfort this new-found piece of information had caused him he said: 'Any more questions?'

'Yes.' A voice from the front. 'If we are not back on the shore after one hour and fifty minutes, how long will you wait?'

It was a thought which had nagged the others, too.

'No. Our whole plan is dependent on the tides. If anyone cannot make the rendezvous in time they will be left behind. But' – and the implications of being stranded at the mercy of the Americans, British and French sank in – 'take comfort in knowing that once on French soil you are only a long train journey away from the Fatherland.

'So if you are somehow delayed and miss the boat – happy onward travelling, my friends.'

There was silence and a few smiles as the men in front of him weighed up the advantages and disadvantages of being nearer to home, but on enemy-held territory. Von Schellenberg shuffled a few papers together on the desk in front of him and prepared to leave. The final briefing was over.

Despite the seeds of doubt Kreiser had tried to sow from the back of the room, the men seemed buoyant, though not over-excited, and von Schellenberg, determining their mood, was pleased by their positive approach to the day ahead. Relaxed conversation, and a few hearty laughs at the expense of the French and Americans, suggested that they were looking forward to their trip to France.

Just one last job to do, and von Schellenberg's role in the Granville raid would be over. 'Oh, by the way,' he said, as he picked up his papers and was about to leave the room. 'I would like to see Vice-admiral Kreiser in my office in five minutes' time.' And without a stiff-armed salute or the prescriptive 'Heil Hitler' he turned on his heels and was gone.

14

Spider's web

PIETER von Schellenberg, Baron Schellenberg of Lotz, Bavaria, ex-commander-in-chief of the occupied Channel Islands and until recently with the power to take or give life to any of the 80,000 people living there, buttoned the top of his leather greatcoat, adjusted his cap smartly and prepared to leave for the car.

Apart from his chauffeur, only his gardener said farewell. With a weary sigh von Schellenberg recognised it was as it should be. Let them keep their damn island if they want it so badly, he thought. And what have I had from them? Four years of their petty squabbling, watching my men become thinner and thinner while they always seem to have that little bit more to eat. Damn their eyes.

But inside he knew it wasn't anger with them he was feeling; it was anger with the way he was being forced to go. He was leaving without being able to see the Granville operation come to fruition. All his planning had been usurped by Kreiser and usurped so completely that even if the raid was a resounding success none of the glory would come his way. A wry smile played on his lips as he recalled Wilhelm Hoffmeister warning him, several days before the disastrous practice run at the Emerald Hotel, that if everything went well, Operation Fahrmann would be a great victory for the Befehlshaber but if it failed miserably he would pay a heavy price.

Operation Ferryman. Von Schellenberg scratched around in his mind for the story he had first learnt at junior school; the Greek legend that – what was it? – that Charon was the son of darkness and of night, ferryman of the dead across the river Styx, taking them to their final abode in Hades' realm. Every passenger paid Charon an obol – whatever that was – so it was customary for the Greeks to bury their dead with a coin in their mouths for the one-way trip from life to death. A coin to pay the ferryman.

It was ironic, von Schellenberg thought, as he bit his bottom lip and shook his head a little at the thought, that in reality he, the ferryman, the instigator of the Granville raid, was paying the cost, not his passengers. He was apprehensive about his return to the wolves of Berlin – wolves, he knew, who were hungry for revenge against all those involved in the failed assassination attempt and hungry, too, for scapegoats like himself, who could be blamed and scorned for their own muddled thinking. Von Schellenberg had no illusions about his sudden recall to Germany. It had been his decision, and his decision alone to mount the Granville raid. Therefore he must suffer the consequences, and the consequences to date had been several men unnecessarily blown up in a Channel Island hotel.

And now, now that he was paying the price it was his rival, Vice-admiral Kreiser, who would reap the rich reward. He knew that if the raid went ahead and – god forbid – went terribly wrong, he, von Schellenberg, would be blamed. But if it went to plan, and was a resounding success . . . The general wiped a bead of sweat from his forehead with the back of his hand as he acknowledged that if all went well it would be Kreiser who would benefit, not he. Damn the man! But he had to admit a sneaking admiration for the way he had been boxed into such a tight corner by the Vice-admiral, who must have been sending a string of telegrams to Berlin over the past few months, every one of them questioning his general's quality of leadership. Well, let Kreiser take over and ferry his raiding party to Granville. He at least would be nearer his beloved Marte back home in Germany.

His eyes levelled out across the garden to the sea and the rocks beyond. Such a pretty little island, he thought to himself. Perhaps, after all, Marte and I will enjoy a holiday here when the war is over. Within an hour of thinking that happy thought he was in a Junkers JU22 and on his way home.

* * * *

THAT last meeting with Kreiser had not been a happy one; not, at least, for von Schellenberg, although he had soon realised that for his rival it was all he could have asked for, all he had been working towards for the last six months.

As the Vice-admiral explained, the islands were now in the capable hands of a naval man – himself – and no matter what happened in this raid tomorrow, they would remain so. Kreiser had gone on to say that he thought operation Fahrmann was an excellent plan, one he was happy to inherit from his predecessor; and there had been a meaningful glint in his eye when he hinted that – for von Schellenberg's sake – he hoped that nothing would go wrong. 'It would be such an awful thing to have to apportion blame,' he said, apologetically, adding that the men had worked hard in training and needed an adventure, a positive performance to keep them happy.

And, he said, although the coal ships meant little enough, the taking of the town even less, it would be a stirring triumph to read of back home as the beleaguered German armies struggled to defend their borders. The icing on the cake of course was Eisenhower – only in that final meeting with Kreiser had von Schellenberg told him of the General's possible presence in the seaside town – but by return Kreiser had said if they *did* bring him back, then he would be kept in the islands every day that the war continued.

Afterwards, once von Schellenberg, poker-faced, had been dismissed from the room, it had been a confident, smiling Vice-admiral Ernst Kreiser who, his eyes moist and shining with triumph, had rubbed his hands in glee and decided, yes, it would be pleasant to enjoy the company of an American general. He looked forward to explaining to General Eisenhower why the Americans should never have allowed themselves to be drawn into this European war in the first place.

15

Forbidden fruit

NIKKI rolled the woman over on top of him again. He had been right about her needing a man. But there had been two weeks of patience; two weeks of gaining first the children's confidence and then Michelle's; two weeks before he had discovered that the way she had shivered when he touched her backbone had not told him a lie.

'She might be a British Army officer's wife, but she is also a woman, a very demanding one,' he reflected, wryly, as he kissed first one breast, then the other, and trailed his hands over her strong, long-backed body.

Smelling of musk and bed, she pushed herself above him, and gazed with quiet approval at his slim, muscled body.

'Who did that to you, Nikki?' she asked, tracing her finger over a jagged red scar which began three inches above his groin and curved slightly, towards his stomach.

'A girl in Amiens,' he said, laughing. 'A very passionate French girl. She was aiming a little lower, perhaps, but in the heat of the moment . . .'

But Michelle Bradwell knew, as he knew, that the scar ran deep and was too regular to be the work of a momentary fit of a French girl's passion.

'Are you always so flippant about life, Nikki? I mean doesn't it bother you that my husband is in France, pushing east to Germany, leading his men against your men, even as we lie here together? That he – and they – will win? Your armies are already retreating, you know, back to Berlin.'

'You and your BBC news,' said Nikki, enjoying the way her hands traced their way down, past the scar, to the inner depths of his thighs.

'So, we lose a war. I have no hatred towards your husband; no, I admire him. Anyone who can marry such a beautiful woman, I admire.

'But I do not admire him for leaving you behind, when there are so many of your needs he should have thought to fulfil, but for marrying you I have nothing but admiration.'

'He would kill you, Nikki, if he knew you were here – in his home, in his bed. He would kill you without any hesitation, just as he kills on the battlefield. He'd probably do it with an awful look of self-loathing on his face – he's always been a bit squeamish. Even when we had a chicken run in Cornwall, and he had to kill and pluck the birds, he'd pull a face – but given the opportunity he'd kill you without a moment's hesitation. He's quiet, and efficient, and takes pride in doing a job well.'

She paused, lost in thoughts that extended across the miles to wherever her husband might be in mainland France.

'I know Philip well enough to know that. He lost his father and elder brother both within a week of each other, not in this war but the last, and I know he would kill you if he had the chance.'

'I could die tomorrow for all sorts of silly reasons,' said Nikki. 'Who knows what tomorrow has in store? But for now, for now I think it is best to enjoy our bodies before they get too old, before no-one wants them. Besides, how do you know he isn't enjoying another woman in some soft French bed?'

Michelle's hands stopped moving, and there was a slightly sadder tinge to her voice as she said, softly: 'No, Nikki. That's not fair. You, and I, we both need a big double bed and a warm body to hold; but not Philip. He will return older, greyer, perhaps, but he always plays fair. Haven't you heard about the

British sense of fair play? He is very correct, very proud, and when I see him again I will scrub you from my mind and pretend you never happened.'

'British sense of fair play,' thought Nikki. 'British sense of fair play,' reminding himself of the photograph of Philip Bradwell on the bedroom dressing table.

The picture showed a sharp-featured man, with a pinched face, high cheekbones, deep-set eyes and thick black, Brylcreemed hair, neatly parted in the middle and combed back from his forehead. He was in uniform and to give the impression that this was a relaxed, informal pose, he held his officer's cap beneath his left arm. It was supposed to be the picture of a man at ease with the world, but despite all the photographer's efforts, the attempt at informality had failed. The officer looked sulkily out of the picture and was holding the cap so tightly he was crushing the material.

Mr Bradwell was a good ten to fifteen years older than his wife, Nick guessed, and his forced smile suggested someone who found it difficult to express his emotions in the company of others – even to his wife. What was that phrase he had heard about the English? – 'cold fish' – that was it, although they made it sound as if the inability to express emotion was something to be applauded. And if, as he suspected, Mr Bradwell really *did* try to play fair in the war, perhaps 'dead fish' was more accurate by now. Playing fair in battle was the silliest occupation he could imagine. He knew that from experience. You don't play fair if you want to survive; you play to win. Just as he had won and bedded Philip's wife. The only rule was – there are no rules.

Nikki was selfish enough to believe that when her husband – *if* her husband – returned, she would not so easily forget her lover's touch. But for now he had other matters of more immediate importance to dwell on. Michelle's busy hands were seeing to that.

The dull ache and – to hell with it – why not? And weighing the English woman's breasts in his hands he rolled her over and sank deeply into her one last time before he would have to get dressed and go to war.

* * * *

'MUMMY, has that German been in your bedroom?'

'No, dear. Why do you say that?'

'It's just that there's a different sort of smell in the room.' said Emma, who couldn't quite explain to herself or her mother why the atmosphere seemed somehow changed.

'You're imagining things, dear,' said Michelle. 'Nikki's just a friend who misses his own wife and children. I would never let him come upstairs into my bedroom – it's for Mummy and Daddy only.'

There was a pause.

'You've looked very pretty since he's started to visit, Mummy. Would Daddy mind him visiting us?'

Mrs Bradwell thought a little before answering.

'Yes, Daddy would. But . . .'

A faltering pause.

'Daddy trusts us, darling, and we have to survive. Nikki has been very kind to us, darling. Don't forget that.'

As Michelle busied herself at the dressing table, looking deliberately in the mirror to avoid her daughter's face, Emma Bradwell stood behind her, one hand resting on the bed's cream counterpane. It was disconcerting to realise that Emma was looking at her curiously, as if seeing her mother in a new light. Feeling guilty and vulnerable, Michelle asked abruptly: 'Don't you like him?'

'Yes. No,' said Emma, surprised by the venom of the question. 'Well, he makes me laugh with his funny accent and jokes. But he frightens me too. Doesn't he frighten you, too, Mummy?'

Michelle looked at herself in the mirror. Even she realised that over the past few weeks she had changed; not only inside herself, but in her looks as well. The frowsty, grey-faced woman of six weeks ago had gone, to be replaced by . . ? She wasn't sure, but she knew she looked healthier, and the thin lines at the side of her mouth had all but disappeared.

'Yes, I suppose he does,' she said, half to herself, as she shook out her hair, and began to coil the thick, brown tresses around her head. 'Yes. He frightens me a great deal.'

16

Ship of the line

PC 411 began her life in the shipyards of the Haarlem River Company Ltd, NY, on 12 April, 1942. She was a 150-foot destroyer whose primary task was to seek out and depth-charge enemy submarines. With a crew of sixty-five, her first task had been as an anti-submarine escort on convoys between Halifax, Nova Scotia, and ports on the southern portion of the eastern American seaboard. Usually the weather was more of an enemy than German submarines during these escort duties, for the PC 411's beam was a scant twenty-eight feet and in stormy conditions she would pitch and roll like a bucking bronco. 'The Bronx Express' her crew called her on such stormy days, although they also used much coarser language – usually with good reason.

On Sunday morning, 30 September, 1943, riding out a hurricane off Cape Hatteras, North Carolina, the slim gunboat very nearly broached and was almost swamped. Three crewmen were washed overboard. None of them should have had a cat in hell's chance of salvation, with waves sweeping high over the bow as the crew tried desperately to ride out the storm, but Fate, and electrician's mate Brad Gorman had other ideas.

The first casualty of the storm was Willie Lomax, who was plucked up and tossed overboard, choking to death in the spume as his horrified shipmates looked on. But Brad Gorman wasn't prepared to watch his friend die. Although Gorman was twice hit by huge waves as he threw out a line – the second wave bowling him along deck before he regained his footing and clung on tight to the guard rail, he was somehow able to haul his friend back to the side of the boat. There he clung on grimly until they were able to scrabble him on board and take him to the warmth of the sick bay below.

For saving Willie Lomax's life, Brad Gorman was awarded the Navy and Marine Corps medal.

But there would be no other medals awarded that day, for as Lomax was reeled in, like a fish on a line, apprentice seaman Paddy Driscoll was drowning. The same wave that took his shipmate caught Driscoll and swept him up and out into the angry sea, drawing him further and further away from the PC 411. Within a minute or so he was lost from sight and was never seen again.

The third man engulfed by the tumult was bosun's mate Jack Telfer, whose chances of survival should have been exactly the same as Driscoll's. But Fate dealt Jack the kindest blow of all that day, for after one wave had knocked him helter-skelter into the sea, the next picked him up and threw him back on board. It was a chance in a million, but he lived to tell the tale.

In the spring of 1944, the Bronx Express was one of several guard boats to a convoy of merchantmen and sea-going tugs bringing pre-cast concrete blocks to Britain. These would be used to make Mulberry harbours on the Normandy coast once the D-Day invasion had begun.

Having crossed the Atlantic, 411's escort duties were over. It was Eisenhower's planning team who ordered her to help escort the US Army's assault force to Easy Red Beach, Omaha section, Normandy, on D-Day, 6 June. The liberation of Europe was about to begin.

Afterwards, with the Allies well entrenched in western France, the ship was again sent to Normandy, this time to act as an escort to coal and supply ships from the UK and as a patrolling gunboat. Part of her crew were rescued and rescuer, for both Gorman and Lomax were still on board, happier that they were sailing in relatively calmer waters as the war in Europe drew slowly to a close. There was no Jack Telfer – he'd decided not to chance his luck and had transferred ship. But here in the Bay of St Malo life – and the seas – were tolerable. There were fewer storms, and although the German Navy had sent a few of their remaining U-boats into the Channel to disrupt supply routes and to cut off and isolate the Allies in France, they were failing miserably. In effect, the hunters had become the hunted, and rarely were U-boats, or any German vessels, seen in this part of the North Atlantic. For Gorman, for Lomax, and for gunner Thomas, sitting behind his 40mm anti-aircraft gun amidships as the ship chugged gently out of Granville Harbour at 9.49 pm on Monday, 8 March, 1945, the horrors of war were nothing much more than a distant memory.

Gunner Thomas liked this part of the world, the Bay of St Malo, with its 40-ft tidal range and its neat little bays, which reminded him of his home in Codshead, Massachussetts, where his main occupation – in between working as a clerk in a bank – had been fishing. He had always been a keen fisherman, which was the main reason he'd volunteered for the navy, not the army or airforce, and although he was many thousands of miles from home, the way he looked at it was that fish were pretty much the same the world over – and he would have given a lot for a line to trail behind the ship. The bass, he'd heard, were particularly prolific in this stretch of water.

Thomas had been on board PC 411 for just over two months, and though he disliked intensely the continual pitching and yawing and the feeling of vulnerability every time they headed out into deep sea, he, like the rest of the crew, shared a grudging love-hate for the ship they were on. It wasn't only the rough and tumble of heavy seas they grumbled about; it was also the economy some bright spark in high office had imposed on the vessel's design, which had led to a second unflattering nickname. The crew also called PC 411 'Old Razor Blade', because the ship's plating was only $^{5}/_{16}$th inch thick. They reckoned you could rip her up with a can opener.

But the ship, unlike many thicker-skinned boats had survived, and gunner Thomas was at peace with the world as they left Granville. Tonight the gunboat would act as replacement guard ship because PC 1003 had a fault with her radar.

As Thomas looked back at the beach and at the lights of the Hotel Normandie flickering into the darkness a mile or so away, he was relaxed, happy to be left alone with his thoughts. In recent weeks blackout restrictions had been broken more and more often, he realised. He was mildly amused by the way that every night a few more householders 'forgot' to draw their curtains, each of them conscious that raids by enemy planes were non-existent and that they could look forward to a quieter world, a return to pre-war normality.

'Join the navy and see the world!' chuckled gunner Thomas aloud to himself, believing that all the seas around him were in Allied hands, and that his job, and the jobs of the pointer and trainer, the two men who made up the rest of his gun crew, were also surplus to requirements. They hadn't fired the gun in anger since he'd joined the ship and he would have been greatly surprised to learn, even as he dreamt of trailing a fishing line, that nearly an hour before, at 8.56 pm, Chips McGovern, a radar operator further up the coast at Coutainville, had located a small fleet of unidentified ships heading east towards the Cotentin peninsula. The officer-in-charge, not unduly worried and thinking it more than likely to be some Allied exercise no-one had bothered to tell him about, agreed it was 'interesting' information, told Chips to pass it on to PC 411 and thought no more about it.

So it was that the information was eventually relayed to 28-year-old Lieutenant James McCabe, USNR, who had been left in charge of the Bronx Express that day. This was McCabe's first command, and when told that three ships were in the area, almost certainly heading south towards Granville or Chausey, his first response was to call up the Allied air base at Cherbourg to ask for air assistance before leaving port to head them off. He wasn't unduly worried to begin with, and took the precaution of alerting the skipper of HM armed trawler Raven, which had arrived at Granville earlier that day and was currently guarding the collier Serendipity in the harbour. 'Come join me,' was the essence of the message, but both the air base and Captain Jackson of the Raven ignored him. So, unaware that there would be no back-up and no reinforcements, PC 411 and its captain and crew went in search of battle alone.

* * * *

ON board the foremost German vessel, the AF 101, which by now had caught up with the minesweepers and swept past them as they made more leisurely progress on their way to Granville, Oberleutnant Matthias Rosenberg was enjoying himself. For too long he and his crew had lived in cramped quarters in St Helier Harbour, rarely, if ever, sailing out from the bay. Today, though, it would be different. Today there would be action. He, too, was a gunnery officer, although he'd only fired once in anger since coming to the Channel Islands, and that had been seven months ago when they'd supported the evacuation of the wounded German troops from the besieged town of St Malo.

He had been afraid that day; it had been daylight, and as well as having to listen and watch as the Americans turned their heavy land artillery on their ships, dropping shells too close to him for comfort, his most vivid memories were of the terrible state of the wounded men as they were carried to the boats from the shore. At the time he was shocked; later came the anger; and now, he believed, it was time for anger to turn to revenge. Instead of retreating, they were finally going to hunt the enemy. As he glanced behind him, where somewhere on the bridge Kapitanleutnant Heinrich Keiffer was directing operations, he felt happier than he'd been for months, and totally unafraid. He had confidence in his commander and also knew, as they all knew, that the Allies were completely unprepared for a raid such as this and that most of the townspeople in Granville would be tucked up in their beds, little realising that their dreams were about to be loudly shattered. All he wanted was the chance to use his 88 mm gun; which, he discovered eighteen years later, was a full 2.8 cm larger than anything the PC 411 had on board. What Matthias Rosenberg also discovered much later, when the war was over and he returned to the islands with his wife and family on holiday, was that his destiny and that of gunner Thomas and his two-man gun crew were inexorably linked together.

* * * *

THROUGH the blackness of the night PC 411 picked up speed and with an increasingly worried captain, followed a course south-west towards Chausey island.

Meanwhile, the three German vessels, knowing the Allied vessel was coming, slowed and waited.

As Matthias Rosenberg picked at his teeth with a nicotine-stained forefinger, the quiet American, Roger Thomas, who enjoyed fishing best of all, looked over the gun barrel to the sea on the port side, realising, perhaps, that something nasty was waiting for them out there, and hating this unexpected trip into the great unknown.

'Two points sou'westerly,' said the Captain, mildly, from the bridge. Married, with a wife and two kids back home in Maine, Lieutenant Jack McCabe did not want to do anything stupid, and was well aware that he could easily be hurrying into a trap. Although the thought of it made the hairs on the back of his neck prickle and brought a thin film of sweat to his forehead, he consoled himself by rationalising the situation. It was inconceivable, he told himself, that there should be any enemy shipping in the area for at least two hundred miles – a U-boat, perhaps, but certainly not three fully-armed German artillery carriers. Where could they come from?

Nevertheless, it was a very worried Lieutenant McCabe who could be seen peering anxiously out to sea from the bridge, suddenly very conscious as they sailed blithely towards whatever lay in store for them that the steel plating which protected his ship was exceptionally thin. The only comforting thought he could manage, the one asset he felt he could rely on if the fleet ahead belonged to the enemy, was the boat's speed – a spanking 35 knots in weather such as this, and a speed available partly because of the ship's slender hull. Of course speed alone wasn't much use in battle; but it was invaluable for getting the hell out of it if everything went wrong.

'We're closing, sir,' said Mullin, the radar operator, picking up three small blips on the edge of the screen, about 5,000 yards away.

'Damn them,' said the Captain. 'Why in blazes don't they identify themselves?

'They must know we're in hot pursuit. Are they the enemy? If so, where on earth have they come from? Any sign yet on the horizon, Larry?'

'No sir. Too dark to see, sir. I guess they're just sitting out there, waiting for us to join the party.'

Radioman Larry Haywood, who had left his radio shack briefly to see for himself what the excitement might be up on the bridge, seemed unworried by whatever lay ahead. Due on leave in six days time, he took everything as it came: war, peace, thunderstorms, sunny days, calm seas. The Good Lord brought them all in turn, just as the Good Lord made certain that no two days were ever the same.

* * * *

12.35 am. The first silhouette of a ship ahead; and in the darkness and nearly a mile away it still seemed massive compared to the sleek 125-foot vessel they were on.

'Jesus Christ!' hissed McCabe . . . just look at that will you. Where the hell did that come from?'

'Artillery carrier, by the look of her. But perhaps it's one of ours,' said second officer Katz. His voice carried no real conviction, and what worried him more than this craft in front of him was that somewhere out there, in the cold waters of the March night, were another two vessels which, for all he knew, were bigger, more heavily armed and all the time getting closer.

'About 1,500 yards, the nearest ship off the port bow,' said Mullin, tracing the blip on the radar as she disappeared from view.

'Tell the gun crews to get ready for one hell of a fight,' said McCabe. 'In two minutes I want six starshells lighting up the sky like it's the Fourth of July all over again. Two minutes, guys, before we either make a fight of it or scoot back the way we came and let the big boys deal with them.'

'You're sure it's Fritz, Lieutenant?' asked Katz. 'Not three of ours making their way south to St Malo?'

'They're German, all right,' said McCabe, more certain than ever that they were waiting for him, waiting for him to make some kind of move before they blew him, his ship and all his crew out of the water. 'But where the hell they've come from, will you tell me?'

Lazily, on the foredeck of the AF 101, the Seeadler, Matthias Rosenberg was training his sights towards what he believed to be the centre of the American gunboat about a mile away, to starboard. Radar had told them where the ship would be, and the only disappointment was the knowledge that only one American ship had been sent to find them. He would have preferred more as target practice and made a conscious note to himself to be as accurate as possible when the first shells were fired. He'd hate to lose this opportunity to test his skill; particularly as he knew that in a few hours time they'd be tucked away in Jersey again, unable, perhaps, to enjoy any other surprise excursions like this into hostile waters.

'One thousand two hundred yards and closing.'

At 00.47 hours, on 9 March, 1945, the sky above the three German artillery carriers was illuminated, as Captain McCabe had requested, as if it were Independence Day. But in lighting up the German gun ships the American flares also lit up PC 411.

'Holy shit – where'd they sneak in from?' thought gunner Thomas, about a minute before the last sound he would ever hear caught his attention.

There was a kind of continuous wheeze, getting louder and louder, then a dullish boom, then a momentary silence before he, and Miller and Drake, were hit.

A clean hit, and a huge smack of pain.

To Miller, looking at where his left arm had been, watching as the blood poured unchecked onto the deck, mingling with the blood of Drake, who was lying a yard away in a mess of jagged metal and tissue, it all seemed so unreal. First the Christmas tree lights and now this.

Another wheezing sound, a hissing, wheezing sound, burrowing quickly through the air. He had learnt quickly what that sound must mean and flinched at the thought.

'Help me, help me!' he screamed, but this time the sound drifted past, this time there was no thud, no flash and explosion. The enemy shell disappeared somewhere behind him.

Out of the corner of his left eye Miller noticed what appeared to be an envelope of flesh flapping loosely where there had once been cheek on bone. And while his right arm dangled ridiculously in front of him, as if owned by a complete stranger, he realised he was still talking, shouting, crying . . . but no, he decided, it wasn't really he who was here in this butcher's shop; it was someone else and this was someone else's terrible dream he had accidentally walked into.

'Please help me, please help me!'

See. It wasn't his voice. It was someone else's, for sure.

'Christ.' One word from above. Harris.

What was he doing here, in this nightmare? It was only a bad dream after all. When he woke up he'd be whole again, wiping sweat from his brow and apologising, with a rather toothy grin, for keeping the others awake at night.

'Harris, Harris, they're cutting me to bits!' his dream told him.

His chest, despite the dream, seemed to be full of pins and needles. Pins and needles; lots of hot pointed pins and needles.

Through the dream Harris appeared strangely real to Miller, and also very businesslike and quite methodical as he ignored the lolling, gaping wounds of gunner Thomas, and the truncated crewman, Drake, smashed to bits by the precision firing of gunner Rosenberg. He ignored them, as best he could. Miller could be saved. Could, if the bastards didn't fire again. That last shell had landed far too close.

'Harris Harris!' the boy screamed again.

'Harris, wake me up from this dream, please, oh God, oh please wake me up from this dream!'

Another man, Haywood, appeared from somewhere in the black of the night. There was a fire in front of him, perhaps on the bridge, but here was only death and the stench of flesh burning.

Harris said something. To Miller it was just a confusion of words as the older man took off his lifejacket and placed it gently beneath his head.

'Harris, what's Haywood doing in my dream? Oh Lord, my pants, I've wet my pants . . .' and his good hand tugged at Harris's sleeve as the other man struggled to his feet to find some blankets to cover the wounded.

For radioman Haywood, watching, the last few minutes had been the worst in his life. Unlike seaman first class Harris, who had been below decks when the the first shell was fired, he had just returned to the radio shack, next to the bridge, when the German artillery ships had opened fire. He, like the rest of the ship's complement, had felt rather than seen the first shell hit home, as the boat shuddered in the night from the impact of German firepower. But it had been the third shell he was to remember the most. First, the ever-loudening wheeze and then the crump as it hit the boat, tearing through the thin sheet metal like paper, tearing with unerring accuracy first into the wheelhouse and then through into the bridge.

Frantically, he had tried to radio for help. It was useless. All contact with the outside world had been lost. Stumbling through the twisted metal he had made his way to the bridge to see what orders the Captain could give, but had stopped, open-mouthed, at the bloody carnage a few yards away from where he'd recently been sitting.

Half an hour earlier he had been joking with his best friend, Robert Mullin. Now only the Captain was left. He had been standing slightly forward and to the left of the others so the shell had ignored him as it struck home. But it had claimed the lives of four of the five people on the bridge or at work in the wheelhouse. If Rosenberg had been a ten-pin bowler he would have been pleased with the score and would have been realigning, looking to pick up the spare.

One quick, heart-stopping look was enough for Haywood. Without entering the blood-spattered remains of wheelhouse or bridge he turned, stepping onto the slippery, lifeless body of Mullin as he did so. He hadn't seen him in the gloom, this slab of meat and tissue lying crooked on the floor, but the knowledge that it was the quietly-spoken Bob Mullin made him violently and physically sick on the spot. Nineteen-year-old Larry Haywood, unused to the proximity of death, turned and fled, not sure where he wanted to go but in some odd, illogical way deciding that as long as he didn't stop running death couldn't overtake him on this cursed ship.

It was as he made his way to the stern that he had heard Miller screaming, and stopped, stunned back into the reality of the night.

Miller's arm was chopped off above the elbow and the left-side of the face, torn away to the bone, was so ugly, so obscene that radio-operator Haywood was mesmerised, unable to look away before Harris, seeing him there, and trying to staunch the flow of blood from Miller's arm, yelled at him to fetch gauze and morphine.

The medical box was behind him, at the rear of the gun-shield. Haywood did as he was told; with no fuss, and with no apparent emotion, unclipping the box and bringing it to Harris's side. 'Christ, you're ugly,' he said to Miller, who looked at him blankly, with wide-open, staring eyes.

It seemed to have been an age since the first, and then the second shell had hit the ship, but in truth only eight minutes had passed since the battle had begun.

With fumbling hands Harris opened the box, took out a length of gauze and tried to tourniquet the arm, but blood kept spurting out until, using a hammer handle, he was able to apply enough force to dam the pressure and turn the flood into a slow trickle. Haywood, conscious that other shells had exploded on or near the ship as he gave Miller first one shot of morphine and then another, scurried away, looking for blankets to provide some kind of warmth for the teenager who was fast sinking into a world of dreams; real dreams this time, in which he believed thousands of tiny black cockroaches were biting into his body while he, like a drunken man, incapable of co-ordination, tried ineffectually to swipe them away.

While Harris and Haywood were doing the best they could to save Miller's life, the ship had been hit twice more, and the sound of running footsteps, of crying and yelling could be heard from virtually every direction. Two small fires had started – both immediately extinguished – although no-one knew what damage had been done below decks. Then, with the ship bucking and riding with no apparent aim or direction, the comforting sound of the two Fairbanks engines which had been taking them away from the gunfire suddenly coughed and died. Rudderless and powerless, PC 411 was at the mercy first of the Germans and secondly of the seas.

If Haywood hadn't stopped to help Harris and Miller perhaps he would have checked his lifejacket and jumped overboard, away from this wreck of a ship. But he didn't; although as far as he was concerned the bridge, the nerve-centre of PC 411, didn't exist anymore. Although he had seen the Captain, briefly, before turning and starting to run, for all he knew no-one was in control and Lieutenant McCabe was now dead – five out of five for the German marksman.

But Lieutenant McCabe, though shocked by the chaos on board, was far from dead. Initially he had tried to steer away from the enemy, talking sweetly to the ship, coaxing, beguiling, while calling the engineers every name he could think of as the Bronx Express lived up to its name by rearing through the Atlantic swell. Then, realising that the steering was dead, he had urged for some kind of manual steering, before discovering that the impact of the explosion to the wheelhouse hadn't destroyed the steering mechanism, it had simply disabled the helmsman.

Mercifully, within a matter of minutes, he had control again, and while the shells continued to rain down on the ship, another one making a huge whole the size of a man's girth through the main deck, landing just above the engine room where it had lodged, he began to guide his command towards France and out of range of those lethal German guns as quickly as he could.

Within a mile of the coast, and approaching the dangerous rocks that surround the pretty seaside town of Cancale, it was at 1.12 am that both Fairbanks diesels stopped completely. An eerie silence, apart from the sound of his own men working or crying, prompted him, calmly and without emotion, to pass the orders to 'stand by to abandon ship', orders which engineer Lomax and able seaman Freekowski, in the charthouse, took with them from the main deck to the cabins below, where the news was greeted with a mixture of reluctance and resignation. The men realised that without power they were sitting ducks; and one or two, deciding that discretion was the better part of valour, chose to jump now, rather than be shelled again later. The sea, they reasoned, was a healthier enemy than the German guns which, although increasingly erratic in line and length, continued to pepper the air and their ship with every kind of shot imaginable. Haywood, however, who chose to stay amidships with Harris and Miller, no longer felt the need to run. Instead he saw everything around him with startling clarity.

'I'm going to die,' he told Harris, who was hunched over the shivering figure of Miller, still trying to patch him up and staunch the bleeding as best he could. 'I'm not going to run away. I'm going to stay here, and die.'

Harris said nothing; but then, what was there to say?

In the remains of the wheelhouse Lieutenant McCabe had also noticed how erratic the German aim had become, and he wondered if this was because, bored with an enemy which refused or couldn't fight back, they were losing interest in such a one-sided contest. Either that, or they were advancing for a kill from point blank range. Whatever thoughts were going through his enemies' minds, he could do no more than pray a little and curse a lot as his ship wallowed helplessly. He hated this silence, knowing that the Germans would know that they had scored more than one direct hit, and that his ship had lost all power.

Then, after a sudden apologetic hiccup, the ship's engines, cleared of the debris that had silenced them, yielded the power he needed to sail a slow course to safety.

As PC 411 limped wearily towards the shore, Kapitanleutnant Keiffer was already turning north, to destroy the lighthouse at Chausey, before making his way back home. As far as he was concerned the American ship was doomed. He'd witnessed its erratic progress after the first few shells had hit, had seen at least a dozen men jump overboard, and had also seen that one of his other ships, nearer to the Americans than his own, had picked up most of them. What was the point in wasting shells on a ship which had no power, no direction, and was perilously close to being swept onto the rocks off Cancale? The Seeadler had been ordered to lure the gunship away from Granville harbour, to destroy it, and to give as much protection as he could to the Granville task force once the raid was over. But 'as much protection' included extinguishing the lights at Chausey, for the darker it remained the better, especially if the airport at Cherbourg were alerted and sent out fighter planes. Within an hour Chausey was in darkness, gunner Rosenberg having enjoyed a second chance to fire his guns that day as he peppered the lighthouse with shot.

As the German ships disengaged from action, picked up the American crewmen who had preferred to take their chances in the water and prepared to sail for Chausey, Lieutenant McCabe on board the holed PC 411, unrecognisable as the fast-moving, uppity 'Bronx Express', was back in complete control. With power and steering restored he had cancelled the order to 'prepare to abandon ship', and sailing as close as he could to the Cancale shoreline, he had steered towards the beach somewhere out there in the inky blackness while ordering a complete report on damage done and people missing. Twelve, he was told, had jumped boat. Eleven were dead. Four were badly wounded, including Andy Miller and Chips Carter, who, from the left side, seemed perfectly whole. It was Carter's other side which had caught the full force of the explosion. He had been on the upper deck when the second shell had touched him, in passing, as it burrowed into the ship. In passing it had also flayed his skin, peeling it to the bone in the same way that the barnacled hull of a boat would peel away flesh when a sailor was keel-hauled in the 18th century. Two hundred years on, the difference was that hot metal could do the job much quicker and with much greater efficiency, as his bloodied head, trunk and leg testified.

Another crew member, motor machinist 2nd class Adie Harben, acting as pointer on the three-inch gun, forward, had, in the same attack been blown out of his gun position in such a fashion that his legs, trapped, beneath the knee, were left behind. What remained was a jagged mix of splintered bone and crushed muscle; two useless adjuncts to his body; but most pain came from the battle-hot shrapnel splinters in his upper torso, in his arms and chest. But Harben, like Carter, lived.

After the vessel was beached and after an hour's wait as Haywood ran desperately first to one house, then to another to seek help without benefit of more than two words of French, Adie Harben still lived. It was to be a painful kind of existence as he came to terms with a wheelchair and an invalid's pension, but thanks to the prompt attention of Dr Le Guyader he returned to America and saw out his three score years and ten.

Not so Andy Miller, who was already turning cold to the touch. He died in the morning of 9 March, 1945, at 5.43 am, despite several attempts to replace lost blood with plasma.

* * * *

1.00 am, 9 March, 1945. In her neat, tidily-kept home in Palace Close Michelle Bradwell and her two children were asleep. Despite the heavy quilt on the bed, and the warm, creamy-pink wallpaper with the small red flowers, the room was cold. Spring, the most unpredictable of seasons, had not yet brought in the sun. One of Michelle's arms snaked over the bed covers to the other side of the bed, where her husband, and in more recent times her lover, had lain with her. Both men were at war; and at the very moment that she turned, moaning slightly in her sleep, not only was Nikki Jagmann in the thick of things, he was loving every minute of it.

17

Major Farthing

IN the Hotel Normandie the remaining members of SHAEF – Supreme Headquarters Allied Expeditionary Forces – were finalising plans to hand over command of the hotel to the new administrators of western France, the United Nations Relief and Rehabilitation Administration (UNRRA), mainly civilians and bureaucrats whose bosses had selected Granville as a base to instruct their personnel before sending them to the war-ravaged areas of Europe they were instructed to control. Although they wore uniforms and a few of them even carried guns, they were trained administrators, not soldiers, whose main role in life was to fill in forms, write letters and make long and detailed telephone calls to other administrators much like themselves.

It was 10 pm, 8 March, and all were working busily, not over-worried about the blackout, knowing that the nearest threat was at least two hundred miles miles east and retreating.

Lieutenant Muskie, one of the soldiers due to head east to join up with the rest of SHAEF the next day, was clearing the desk where he'd been working, and was looking forward to a good night's sleep before setting off at daybreak first for Rennes and then on to Poitiers. It had been a busy day; up since 6.30 am to welcome the second batch of UNRRA people, many of them looking decidedly unsoldierly as they left the train, their nervous excitement at being inside recently-occupied France apparent as they chattered to him about their working brief.

It was Lieutenant Muskie's task to show them the town and to introduce them to the mayor and other members of the municipality, and although he hated this, the formal, petty bureaucratic side of war, and the constant jostling for position in the administrative hierarchy, he was a realist; the war was ending, and for the sake of his own career he needed to accept, and be good at, this other type of battle. Besides, he had seen plenty of action since coming ashore at Utah beach on 7 June, 1944, twenty-four hours after 155,000 Allied troops had begun the D-Day Normandy offensive to reclaim France from Germany; and although he looked younger than his twenty-four years, with an engaging smile and an almost apologetic way of explaining things to his UNRRA guests, he had witnessed more death in action than they would ever know. He might have been a day late for the landing, but in helping to take Colleville-sur-Mer, and in the prolonged fighting afterwards as the Allies reclaimed Normandy, mile upon bloody mile, he had lived through some of the most ferocious fighting that France had ever seen. The men with their briefcases and wire-rimmed glasses, the secretaries with their smart hair-dos and lipstick, and the dark-suited men with their trilbys and agitated manner, would have been shocked if they had seen the same soldier eleven months ago, pouring bullets into a German gun emplacement and urging his men not to let any of the bastards escape from the trench alive.

The bastards didn't – but then by that time he had passed the stage of philosophising or moralising about war. He'd seen enough of his own men cut to ribbons, their bodies dragged away to allow the next wave of men the opportunity to gain a few more yards, unhindered by corpses lying across their path. And afterwards, when they'd met up with the Brits at Colleville and continued their attack to Bayeux, and on to Caen, only then had he been able to assess his reaction to the business-end of war and to realise, with something approaching shock and with a sense of profound self-disgust, that he'd quite enjoyed it; not the waiting, nor the digging-in deep in foxholes, but the power a gun gave you over who might live and who might die.

The first time, when he'd fired a gun from almost point blank range and claimed his first victim of the war, that had been the test, he realised, looking back on the killing a day or so later. The first time, like the first real kiss, would live with him always. But not the other men; not the second or third man, both of them cut down not with a gun but by grenade; not the fourth, fifth or sixth man raked by rifle fire . . . and by the end of the second day of battle he had steeled himself sufficiently to be able to return to the enemy, to turn him over with the toe of his boot and to look carefully at his eyes. If they were sightless he might wonder what sort of man he had been, but only with the detached interest of, say, the coroner, after foul play had been suspected and an inquest was ordered. If, on the other hand, the eyes flickered with life, he would take careful aim and fire again. It wasn't hate, or anger, he told himself, but compassion which steadied his arm as he fired that second bullet. He saw it as his duty; to put a wounded animal out of his misery, just as he would prefer an honourable death on a battlefield rather than being patched-up and institutionalised, put in a home where your shattered body excited the same emotion from friends and family alike – the one emotion he couldn't bear: pity. He could not live in a broken body and he could not live a lifetime of pity. He shivered uncomfortably at the thought.

'Lieutenant,' a voice caught him unawares, as he was reaching across the table to put the last set of maps in his bag. 'Lieutenant, this is Major Farthing. Lieutenant Muskie – Major Thomas J Farthing, US Land Division, No 9'.

'Always so damn formal,' thought Lieutenant Muskie, after the mumbled hello and a handshake.

'Call me Mike,' he said, releasing his hand – a soft handshake, he thought, as he weighed up the Major in his immaculate uniform and starched-collar shirt.

'Major Farthing will be looking after the UNRRA guys over the next few days before they leave for Rennes,' explained Lieutenant-colonel Mark Anderson, commanding officer of the forty-two remaining American soldiers who had been quartered in the Hotel des Ormes, in Granville's old town. 'After Rennes they'll be moving on throughout western France and the Major hopes to catch up with us a few days later at Mamedy. He's from your neck of the woods, Long Beach, I believe. Perhaps you know each other.'

No, they didn't know each other. Long Beach California was larger, more sprawling and diverse than Lieutenant-colonel Anderson imagined, and Muskie realised, after a moment or two of conversation, that they were from two different sides of the same town. The Major had gone to St Joseph's, a fee-paying school which the rich kids attended, before moving on to Yale. His had been a tougher upbringing in County High. But they passed a few minutes amicably enough, as both sought to establish common ground for conversation.

'What's the General like?' asked the Major, after they'd gone through a list of mutual friends they might have had, but didn't.

'General Eisenhower?' replied Muskie. 'A hard man but a fair man.' There was a pause. He could have added that the General was more a soldier than a politician, and that he'd never seen him in a smart dress uniform like that worn by the Major, Ike preferring clothes for comfort and warmth rather than effect. Instead he said: 'He takes some getting used to, doesn't suffer fools gladly and he's a stickler for detail; but I'd prefer him on my side than theirs any day. The men like him, and have confidence in him, probably because he's a tough old bird and doesn't underestimate the intelligence of the enemy.

'All he's interested in right now is to win this war and to wrap it up as quick as he can.'

As he said this to the Major he couldn't help but smile inwardly to himself, comparing the man in front of him, with his soft handshake and well-cut uniform, to Ike Eisenhower, who wasn't worried by image, who looked every part a soldier and was, without question, a leader of men.

When Ike had left the hotel three weeks ago he had told this young Lieutenant he'd come to like that they'd meet up next in Berlin, where perhaps they'd share a bottle of German wine together. It had been said with genuine conviction; and although Lieutenant Muskie would never admit that he could ever *like* anyone who controlled his destiny – he preferred to leave that option open for himself – with Ike he felt somehow reassured, as if through all the impossibilities of war they *would* meet again.

It was now 10.25 pm, a reasonable enough a time to say good night to this brand-new Major in his brand-new uniform.

'The town's all yours, Major,' Lieutenant Muskie told him, as he picked up his jacket and cap, ready to leave. 'And oh,' he added, before leaving. 'Just a thought. If you've got a good imagination, my advice to you is not to go all the way up to the top floor. Your mind can play some pretty mean tricks on you if you do.' And with that he was gone.

'What kind of a remark was that?' said the Major to Colonel Anderson, as Muskie, head bowed and shoulders hunched, walked into the Granville night air, towards the Hotel des Ormes. 'If you've a good imagination your mind can play mean tricks.'

'Ignore it for today, Major,' said Anderson, realising that Muskie and Farthing hadn't hit it off the way he'd expected. 'I'll take you up and show you what he was hinting at tomorrow. These days there's nothing there but wooden floors and empty space.'

That 'these days' suggested that this hadn't always been the case – and when the Major hauled his way up two flights of stairs to the uncomfortably soft bed and the hard, sausage-shaped bolster, he decided that first thing tomorrow he would find out for himself exactly what secrets the Hotel Normandie held at the top of the house.

* * * *

THE town of Granville is, in effect, two towns. The High Town, La Haute Ville, the older part, was built on a rocky peninsula, reaching out in a V-shape west towards the sea. At the furthest point the French had built a watch tower and small lighthouse which had been added to by the Germans. First, they built a radar scanner, and then not one but two bunkers, the second still housing a P52 gun which the French or Americans might have been tempted to use when they regained control of the town, had they had any ammunition to use with it.

The Allies controlled the radar station, and had a direct link from there to Cherbourg, the radar operator living in a newish house beneath the radar and radio equipment in a large hollow cut away in the rock. From the windows of his home he could see the small square inner harbour to the south; much more sheltered than the open expanse of white sandy beaches running as far south as the eye could see. Beyond the inner harbour was the outer harbour which, at low tide, drained rapidly, leaving the few tiny fishing boats and the two British colliers moored there firmly embedded in silt and mud.

Three hundred yards inland from the radar station, and dominating La Haute Ville's southern slope, was a large granite church and an even larger granite building two doors away, westwards. Both had been built nearly two hundred years before. The first pointed upwards, a tribute to God; the second, a three-storey edifice, reached across and down, a tribute to no-one. This was the barracks; a functional building with barred windows, through which generations of French soldiers had looked on the port below. Used as a storehouse by the Germans, it had reverted to its proper use and for thirty or so Frenchmen it was, and had been for five months or more, home.

Only one road, the Boulevard des Amiroux, zigzagged its way to La Haute Ville from the south-east and the 'new' town. It ended in a small market place at the top of the hill.

Further to the north the land fell sharply away to the sea and to a clean, sandy beach which locals and tourists had flocked to regularly each summer before the war. Separating the beach from dry land was a high sea wall and, behind this, a promenade, which curled inland near the Hotel Normandie to the new town and its many narrow streets and shuttered houses.

There was no immediate path between the the old town to the hotel – you had to go slightly inland first, and then approach La

Haute Ville from the south, along the Boulevard des Amiroux – but because it was the only large building above the beach, taller, even, than some of the nearby cliffs, it demanded attention. Immediately in front of the hotel, on reclaimed waste ground, was a large car park and, two streets away, on the Rue Bechélet, which connected the Hotel Normandie with the Boulevard des Amiroux, was the Hotel des Ormes, in the middle ground between the old town and the new. This was where most of the American soldiers were stationed.

The Germans had done their homework well. The first task they had set themselves was to cut off the high town from the rest of Granville, which could be simply done if first they took control of the only road which took you there. By taking the Boulevard des Amiroux they would also be isolating the Hotel Normandie, although one of their priorities was to take control of the radar and communications centre, to prevent the outside world from knowing what was happening. With La Haute Ville and the Hotel Normandie cut off they could deal first with the Americans, who they recognised as the main threat to their ambitions, then with the French, who, they believed, would be very loathe to move out of their barracks if every time they came to the door a burst of machine gun fire was sprayed in their direction.

And, while the French and Americans were being dealt with by men of 619 Division, a small fleet of minesweepers would be stealing through the port, searching out colliers and any large ships that could be hijacked and taken back to Jersey.

It was a meticulously researched plan, depending very much on the information supplied to von Schellenberg by the five men who had made their escape from Granville eight months before. There were also subtleties von Schellenberg and Colonel Hoffmeister had insisted on, including the decoy run by the three AF ships from Granville to Chausey and the support from two artillery carriers which would be offshore at Le Nec, the rocky outcrop where the radar station had been built. The ships' guns would be aimed towards the centre of the new town, ready to shell indiscriminately if anything went wrong.

But there were to be changes. Ernst Kreiser, though pleased by the scrupulous preparation and the eagerness of the men under his command to go to war, could not allow Hoffmeister to take command. It must be seen as a naval victory – if all went well. Besides, Hoffmeister had been a personal friend of the disgraced von Schellenberg, now kicking his heels somewhere in Berlin, and his loyalty was questionable. Oberstleutnant Karl von Mannstein, on the other hand, could be relied upon implicitly to do exactly as he was told. He lacked the colour and force of personality of the bear-like Colonel, but he would do nothing to harm his Admiral's career. True, by demoting Hoffmeister Kreiser ran the risk of alienating the other men in 619 Division, who would view any last-minute changes by a naval man with great suspicion, but he hadn't climbed so far, so quickly, without learning the potency of a few quiet words, spoken in earnest at an appropriate moment.

A few hours before the task force assembled in St Helier Harbour Kreiser had taken Hoffmeister into his confidence.

'I need you to help me solve a problem,' he began. 'Jagmann. I have every faith in him as a soldier, and as a leader of men, but . . .' and he trailed away, looking to see how Hoffmeister would react to what he had said.

Hoffmeister didn't react; or rather he continued to look at the new Commandant in the same guarded way.

His subordinate's refusal to ask: 'But what?' annoyed Ernst Kreiser, but instead of showing his annoyance he said: 'I feel he is too inexperienced to lead the raid on the Hotel Normandie. We can't afford any slip-ups – nothing must go wrong, especially if we hope to capture this American general. It could be argued, of course, that at this late stage we shouldn't make any last minute changes; but I want to make this one, at least. I want you to lead the raid on the hotel. I would feel a lot more confident knowing that you were in command. I value your experience and your judgement . . .' and once more his voice trailed away, allowing Hoffmeister to reflect on the implications of this double-edged persuasion. Demoted – yes. But demoted to fulfil the real task of

Operation Fahrmann, to bring back Eisenhower to the islands. If he refused, and if Jagmann failed, he would suffer the consequences of having turned down Kreiser's request. It might well be that this was an off-the-record chat, a search by Kreiser for a solution to a difficult problem, but as soon as anything went wrong, especially if it went disastrously wrong, it would become common knowledge, and already Hoffmeister could hear the Vice-admiral complain: 'I warned the Colonel that I was concerned about Lieutenant Jagmann. I told him he was too inexperienced and that it would be best if he led the raid, but he said "no".' Better, therefore, to put a brave face on it and see it as a vote of confidence in his own skills as a military man; better to say 'yes, I will bring you back your prisoners', knowing that if he failed, he was placing his own head on the block. Kreiser, and through Kreiser Berlin, would punish failure as ruthlessly as they would award themselves the plaudits and garlands of victory if the battle were won.

So Hoffmeister said 'yes' – which didn't please Jacob Kesselring, who was told he would now become Hoffmeister's second in command and that Lieutenant Jagmann, unaware of the question mark against his name, would lead the attack on the Hotel des Ormes. As far as Jagmann was concerned, one hotel was very much the same as any other. As long as there were enemy inside waiting to be killed he was happy.

The final change in the jigsaw was to give Otto Lindenheim command of the two ships, FL17 and M160, which were to remain outside the harbour to provide covering fire if needed. Captain von Mannstein had already been told that he would be on the lead ship, in overall charge of the Granville raid.

Afterwards, an hour before the small flotilla left the harbour, the Vice-admiral wished his men well and, from the deck of his gunboat proferred a stiff salute before sailing for Guernsey, where he would spend the night in one of the underground rooms in the radio bunker at St Jacques. If all went well he would hear nothing. He had ordered a complete radio curfew unless the raid went disastrously wrong. Only when von Mannstein was close to home would radio silence be broken. And afterwards, if all had gone well, it was to be hoped at around 6 am, Kreiser would be able to let Berlin know that they – he – had achieved a famous victory.

Meanwhile, as he waited in the sparsely furnished ante-room underground at St Jacques, wiling away the minutes by drinking cup after cup of weak black coffee, the Granville raid, Operation Fahrmann, was out of his hands. It would be foolish to pretend that he wasn't concerned that the raid might go wrong; but he consoled himself that if it were a disaster, it would not be his fault. It might be Hoffmeister's, or von Schellenberg's, who would be 'credited' with planning the raid, but it would not be his. He would accept only victory. Anything else just wouldn't do, and he relied on Karl von Mannstein to apportion blame accordingly if the enemy proved too strong and if the task force had to scuttle back to the islands in defeat.

It was important than von Mannstein was there, Vice-admiral Kreiser decided, as he sipped his fourth – or was it his fifth? – cup of coffee. So far the only person he had spoken to had been the radio operator, Helmut Sterne. They had had brief conversation before he'd returned to his room where he was picking his way through von Schellenberg's book, 'Besetzung der Kanalinseln'. It amused him to read it knowing that the author of such elegant prose was almost certainly arguing for his life in beleaguered Berlin, although in his own nervous excitement he was finding it increasingly difficult to concentrate. His mouth was dry and he was conscious that his shirt was damp with sweat. He looked at his watch: 01.30. The raid would be under way by now. No time for turning back. He turned another page.

18

Stick in the mud

IT was 1.34 am and Karl von Mannstein was a happy man, in many ways the happiest he'd been since he'd arrived in the islands. He had not expected to be included in the Granville raid and, indeed, had sneered at it when he discovered that Hoffmeister would be in charge. But, given the opportunity to command not only the entire operation once they left St Helier Harbour, but to command Hoffmeister as well, he was puffed up with his own self-importance. This is how it was meant to be; a night of action, in which the Americans and the British would see another side of the German character, resilient and resourceful to the end.

So far he could not have wished for a better start to his adventure. The crossing from Jersey to the Cotentin peninsula had gone exactly as planned, with no hiccups and with each of the support vessels playing its part to perfection. The night had been so dark you could imagine cutting it into slices, and yet when they met a mile outside Granville, each ship arrived exactly on time. Already the AFs had set sail for Chausey, leaving the way clear for the minesweepers to drop Jagmann's commandos in their boats about 800 yards out from the north beach. Hoffmeister was to follow in the second wave of attack five minutes later.

Although von Mannstein had made a point of wishing Jagmann well, it had been Hoffmeister who had had the last word, thumping Nikki on the back in a hearty farewell and reminding him that he should ignore the French wine and bring back with him at least one bottle of apple brandy, possibly two, the traditional drink of the Normandy people.

'Burns your throat and brings tears to your eyes,' he had joked, as Nikki returned his smile and saluted lazily, his thoughts already racing to the work ahead. Within a few minutes of bidding farewell he was in the boat, crouched alongside twenty-three other men, proud that he, and they, were going ashore together to wage war on the enemy. Nikki smiled inwardly as he looked at his comrades; fine, fighting men, the tools of war, already so in tune with each other that only the most vigilant of observers would have seen the occasional flash of a paddle cutting through the water. Eight men soundlessly propelled the boat, the others, heads down, were equally silent.

As they pulled strongly to the shore he heard the muffled 'plash' of Hoffmeister's dinghy behind and was comforted by the sound. There would be eighty-one commandos in all in four craft, each one making good and even progress through the rolling sea. Eighty-one commandos . . . one large landing party which would then divide into smaller groups, each with a specific purpose, each a cog in the German machine, to make certain the town would fall.

The first, and the smallest group of all, led by von Bastion, would immediately head through the town to Le Nec to destroy the radio and radar centre. The less communication there was with the outside world the better. Then, as thirty-six troops climbed the beach to take the Hotel Normandie, the remainder would scatter through La Haute Ville, one party to take the Hotel des Ormes, another to surround the French barracks on the other side of the hill, another to begin, five minutes later, shooting indiscriminately in the streets to add to the confusion and to ensure that the French townspeople stayed in their homes. The last thing they wanted was an unruly crowd of patriotic Frenchman rallying to the defence of their town.

Nikki was part of the main group, which by now had skirted

round the Hotel Normandie towards the old part of the town. As von Bastion and his men hurried on past the church and the German-built bunkers to the very tip of the old town to Le Nec, his first priority was the Boulevard des Amiroux, the road leading between the old town and the new. They'd decided against barricades or a large force of men to defend the road – what reinforcements could the Allies muster and where would they come from? But just as it was important that no-one should cross into the old town to find out what was happening, so it was vital that no-one should leave La Haute Ville to sound the alarm and explain exactly what was happening. Five men were therefore detailed to hide in shop doorways to cover the boulevard; another twenty were sent to deal with the French barracks with orders to shoot anyone who so much as poked his nose out of a window; the remainder stole, as quickly and as quietly as they could, to the Hotel des Ormes. Jagmann, in the lead, would rejoin Hoffmeister in the Hotel Normandie once he had dealt with the Americans.

As he and his men made their way through the deserted streets the first attack on the harbour on the other side of the hill was about to begin.

* * * *

AT around 1.25 am the M62, the M57 and the auxiliary minesweeper M343 entered port, the last two coming alongside ready to put landing parties ashore to carry out demolition work after the harbour had been raked with fire from 2 and 3.7 cm cannon. The fire was not only designed to destroy as many of the cranes and as much of the rolling stock as possible, but also as another reminder to the good people of Granville that this wasn't a sensible time to climb from their beds to find out what was happening.

As all three ships searched out the colliers they knew were either inside the port or in the outer harbour, von Mannstein smiled with delight as he saw, in the glow from the burning ruins of the port installations, his men running along the harbour wall, barely stopping to place an explosive before continuing to run to the next piece of machinery; always two men, one in front, one behind, to protect the third, middle member of the group who carried the explosives.

Fifteen minutes had elapsed since they had entered the harbour and not one retaliatory shot had been heard, although von Mannstein could hear the sound of gunfire in the old high town. Everything, he realised, was going to plan; in fact better than planned, for they had calculated that they would almost certainly be slowed down by some kind of spirited resistance. But no. The harbour, it would appear, was theirs.

They had another hour to go before they would have to cut and run; a timescale which had been decided for them by the rise and fall of the tide. By 3 am the sea would have fallen dramatically, and although this would not have mattered before the war, when the French port authorities had regularly dredged the thick mud and sandbanks in Granville harbour, it mattered in 1945, three years after they had last been cleared.

While the small, flat-bottomed coal-carrying ships arriving from England had managed to unload their cargo in the harbour, their captains were wary of the port, and often preferred to anchor further out in the bay, in deeper waters, once they had unloaded. So for Captain von Mannstein, aware of the dangers and aware, too, that the tide began to flow rapidly at 2.30 am, there would be no second chance if any members of the raiding party were late returning to the boats. He could not afford for any of his ships to be stranded on a sandbank or marooned by the tide. At ten minutes to three he would return to Jersey. Stragglers would be left behind.

With the greatest trepidation, von Mannstein guided the deep-keeled M62 through the outer sea defences and into harbour. As he grew accustomed not so much to the dark but to the sounds of the battle, first in the north of the bay, then in La Haute Ville, a flush of pride glowed deep in his heart. This was his expedition, his war, and his men looked to be winning as efficiently and as methodically as he had been told they would.

It was now his turn to go into battle. He ordered his men to take his ship that little bit further into harbour and his heart quickened as he anticipated the part he would play in the war. Already his two companion vessels were part of the action, and while the guardship, the Raven, had been taken within a few minutes of their stealthy approach into port by Schillinger on the M57, the collier Serendipity was only now being boarded, the crew in for a rude awakening as they discovered they had German troops for company.

The boarding vessel currently playing at pirates was the M343, which had moved smoothly alongside the Serendipity. Oberleutnant Schlegel had been the first man to climb aboard the grubby little coal ship, stoker Watkins the first man to greet him as he climbed up on deck. Surprised by this man in a dark uniform climbing over the side and not fully awake to the fact that the semi-automatic he was carrying meant that he meant business, Watkins was more angry than afraid. Angry that his sleep had been disturbed by such a noisy carry-on.

'Bugger off,' he said, as Schlegel swung a foot over the side of his ship.

The German, who didn't understand a word of English, but recognised the tone, swung one leg, two legs over the side of the coal ship and promptly had to dodge the man's laboured attack with a shovel. If it had connected, his skull would have been smashed. But it didn't connect, and without wanting to waste any time in disarming this clumsy oaf, Schlegel did the simplest thing, and did it well. He aimed his gun with precision and fired.

'Always aim for the largest target,' he had been told. 'The largest target provides the best chance of success.'

So he did just that; without counting on the scream or the look of horror or, indeed, on the impact as, fired from two yards, the bullets tore into stoker Bernie Watkins' stomach and dumped him backwards, like a huge floppy doll, his belly exploding.

The stoker's intended scream was stifled by blood spilling out from his throat as Schlegel looked on in curiosity at what he'd just accomplished. The challenge, counter-challenge and death had happened in less than thirty seconds, and as he carried on across the deck to the companionway he felt slightly in awe at what he'd just been responsible for. He'd never killed a man before. For days afterwards the sight of that large, bearded Britisher, with eyes that seemed to be popping out of his head as he was jerked backwards, lived in his dreams. He just couldn't grasp how suddenly that human grizzly bear had been turned into a 210-lb piece of meat.

But now it was time which was important; the time it took to climb below to the crew's quarters. He was conscious that he had been joined by two of his men, both as eager as he to hijack this boat and take it back to Jersey.

Below decks there were two more British sailors; men who at first weren't afraid of the guns pointed in their direction, but angry and upset that their sleep had been disturbed.

'What the hell do you want?' one of them had asked – a reasonable request at half past one in the morning.

'Up on deck,' Schlegel told them, in German, and although neither crewman could understand a word of what was being said, the guns rather than the language encouraged them to move without any hint of rebellion. Like Bernard Watkins they might well have been angry, but they weren't so daft that they would argue with three heavily-armed German soldiers, and if they had to sit out the rest of war as prisoners – then that was it. It made more sense than being shot and thrown overboard as hors d'oeuvres for the fish.

Other members of the crew were being brought up as Anton Schlegel ushered his prisoners to the main deck. They included three Liverpudlian navvies, yawning and scratching, and a scrawny Scotsman who, in dirty vest and longjohns, was cursing under his breath and holding his hand, which looked to be broken.

'I had to hit him with the gun barrel,' explained Muller. 'He wouldn't do as I asked although I told him twice. It was only tobacco he was reaching for, but how was I to know that? So I hit him. Twice. Very hard.' And he gave the man a smile, as if to show that there were no hard feelings about his busted hand.

Tommy McCain wasn't in the mood for reconciliation. His hand hurt him too much, and as he followed the rest of the crew members dutifully on deck, it was obvious by the black looks he gave his captors that he was not a happy man.

With one man dead, and another seven captured, the collier was now under German command, and as the ship was searched from stern to bow for other men who might have slipped away from the cabin in an attempt to hide, the six Englishmen and one Scot were told – or rather made to understand by the unsmiling Germans – that for them, at least, the war was over. They and their ship had become prisoners of war, explained Schlegel to the man with the broken hand.

He presumed this to be the captain or at least their commanding officer, because of the way the other Englishers had looked to him as they waited on deck, although it was quite inconsequential who was in command now they had taken the ship. Perhaps the Englishman hadn't quite understood what he had tried to say; perhaps he was just an angry fool; either way he had carried on protesting for far too long before Muller, after a curt nod of the head from his commanding officer, had hit him hard across the face with his rifle butt.

'Some people will never learn,' he said to himself as the captured crew were taken below, where they were securely locked in one of the larger cabins. He could sympathise with their sudden reversal of fortune but then this was war, where you were taught always to expect the unexpected – even if, tucked away in a French harbour, many miles away from the boundaries of frontline fighting, you had better reason than most than to believe that you could sleep soundly in your bunk, knowing that the next day you would be returning to England.

But now, now they would be making a much shorter journey and, Lieutenant Schlegel realised, with a ghost of a smile, they would not know why, or where.

With the engines running and the anchor hauled up, the Serendipity set sail for Jersey, crewed by Germans. Her cargo? Apart from fuel oil to power the ship the hold was empty. But they'd captured a ship, six English seamen, one grumpy captain and, currently forgotten in the black of the night, a corpse, still leaking blood and lying spread-eagled over a tarpaulin near the stern on the main deck.

Captain von Mannstein had seen Schlegel and his men board the Serendipity as his own boat, the M62, moved silently past them, towards the largest collier, the Devonia, sitting idly at her moorings, a honeypot ripe for licking. For the Captain this was to be a moment to savour: the moment when, after so many wasted days in tranquil waters, where the only adventure had been the unenviable delight of acting as a ferry between islands, he would engage his ship in action. He was proud of tonight, proud of his Fatherland and proud that it was to be his victory. In his mind's eye he was already enjoying the praise, the backslapping, all received with the same self-effacing 'please . . . no . . . it was nothing', while he wondered, even as the boat steamed further into the harbour, which medals he would win. Behind him, to the north, the light of the small lighthouse on the old town peninsula might long have been extinguished, but he could still hear the sporadic sound of gunfire, which suggested that the radar station had not yet been taken. On the quayside the last few fuses were being primed, with no retaliation.

If the army were doing as well in the old town as the navy were doing in harbour, Ernst Kreiser would be delighted. Why, if all went well, it might even give new heart to the forces back home, besieged, out-numbered, despairing of their Führer but fighting passionately for their homeland. And, if Eisenhower could be brought back alive, perhaps the war could, indeed, be shortened. Better to lose to the Americans than the Russians and better still to negotiate from a position of strength. In that he shared von Schellenberg's view: with the right hostages they might lose the war but win the peace.

By now his ship was the furthest inshore; almost too far, he decided, as he ordered her to go alongside the coal ship Devonia. He looked at his watch. Another forty-five minutes and they would be on their way home. With three Allied ships taken prisoner and the greatest catch of all, an American general stowed safely below, it would be a night to savour.

What Karl von Mannstein did not know, however, as his ship approached the Devonia, anchored in the middle of the harbour, was that while the waters to the west, south and north of the M62 were deep, and clear of silt, to the east – where there should have been the deepest waters of all – there lay the hulk of a small crabbing boat which for the past two months had been rotting away, gradually silting over. No-one had bothered to remove her – why should they? The colliers could pass easily over her at high tide, and in months to come, when the silt was so thick it could jeopardise their journeys to the harbour, the war would be over. The French authorities could then clear the vessel and the harbour at their leisure.

It was easy for Vice-admiral Kreiser, later, to accuse his commanding officer of being over-ambitious, and of acting without due care but in truth this was a lie. So when the wrenching sound from below, and the jolt, followed by the uneasy feeling that the sea was no longer deep beneath them told Captain von Mannstein the sickening news that they had hit the bottom – and stuck – it was not his fault that this was the case. It was fate, or poor fortune, which had intervened.

According to the German handbook neither of those f-words existed: didn't you make your own good luck by careful preparation, so nothing untoward could happen, so nothing could go wrong? But for the Captain the ensnaring of the M62 marked the end of the war in bitterest fashion.

Not that he was to know this, as he demanded to know what was happening.

'We've touched bottom, sir. The propeller is fouled in the mud,' a frightened rating told him, alarmed by the red-faced anger of his superior.

'All power. Reverse engines.'

But no; reverse engines as much as they would, it made no difference. The ship was well and truly aground.

It was no consolation to von Mannstein that the Devonia was only a few yards away, offering an open invitation to be boarded. And when they looked inside her hold, discovering that most of the coal remained and would prove of great value to the islands, what should have been excellent news was received with no more than a curt: 'Good. I see.' For try as they would, they could not, in the time remaining, float the minesweeper, either by lightening her load or by attempting to pull her away with a combination of her own and the Devonia's less-than-powerful engines. The wrecked crabber, and the silt, held her tight. The more power they applied, the more the silt swirled around the keel, pulling her in deeper. Within half an hour von Mannstein had no choice but to order his men to abandon ship as he transferred his command to the smaller, dirtier British coaling vessel. Already the tide was draining away, and the euphoria he had felt such a short time before had been replaced by bitterness and frustration.

As he ordered the scuttling of his ship and watched his men place explosive charges in the hold to ensure she would sit out the rest of the war trapped in harbour, he was silent, unapproachable and wrapped in a depression it would be heartless to describe. And when he returned to his new vessel of command, his mood was not helped by each of the five British crewmen, now prisoners on the Devonia, who part-answered his questions about Granville's defences with insolent grins and comments about the 'mighty German Navy' which didn't require translation. They knew he'd run aground and had swapped a fair vessel for a foul. As the clock ticked away the only consolation he allowed himself was the knowledge that Hoffmeister, who should have led the assault on Granville, not he, might be late for the boat.

'I hope they all get shot to hell,' he said, unreasonably, as he looked out from the smaller vessel to the larger one, as the sound of an explosion below decks tore through the night. 'And if they think I'm going to wait one minute after 02.50 hours they've got another think coming,' he added, for good measure.

19

First wave

ON shore – on the French mainland – Nikki Jagmann was in his element. Sleeping with women was a great ten-minute feast but nothing could compare with the excitement of pitting yourself against the possibility of death.

At times like these the wound along his belly would always ache a little, a reminder that it was best to act first, justify the action second. It had not been a lover's tiff and a blade wielded by a jealous girlfriend which had savaged him, but the knife of a Canadian airman who had parachuted over Amiens nearly three years before, the man hanging like some silly puppet from a tree as Nick, believing he was incapable of anything except surrender, had tried to cut him down.

The silly fool had resisted – and lunged.

The downward thrust had hurt Nick's pride more than his body, he remembered, because as a professional soldier he should have anticipated it coming. Even now he wasn't sure, if that lunge hadn't been made, whether or not he he would have cut the Canadian down and taken him prisoner or whether he would have put him out of his misery by shooting him there and then as he hung so disconsolately from the tree. After such a stupid attack, of course, he had no choice. He had stepped back three yards before firing twice, aiming at the head, before leaving the corpse to rot as dead meat for the crows.

After Nikki's wound had healed he never again took chances.

'In war the only rule is that there are no rules,' became his favourite saying, and it had proved a valuable guideline not only for himself, but for many of the other men he had led into battle since they'd sent him back to war.

And here he was, eighteen months since his last skirmish with the enemy, leading men into battle again. It seemed a little unfair that it had been such a long time coming, and because it might be a long time before the opportunity was repeated, he determined to enjoy it, and to lead his men well.

Leaving Heinrich Wolfe in charge of the men covering the Boulevard des Amiroux, he led the remaining twenty-four soldiers under his command towards the Hotel des Ormes. There was an outside chance that Eisenhower, the American general, would be sleeping there, with his fellow Americans – but he doubted it. He supposed that American generals slept in four-star hotels like the Hotel Normandie, which was currently under attack from Hoffmeister and Lindenheim. The point was, however, that it didn't matter any more: for this was the excitement, the adventure of going into the great unknown, where you had some kind of plan but where you never knew what might be hidden around every corner.

Without needing to look round he knew that the other men were close behind as he headed swiftly, silently, through the deserted streets, and without needing to look at his watch he judged that they were a minute or so ahead of schedule.

Everything was going to plan as he counted his men towards the hotel, urging them on as they fanned out around the high walls, each man with a given task and a given time to complete it. This was the first part of the plan of attack: in unison the leading men were to take control, simultaneously breaking through the main front door, a back door and a side window, which was to be smashed open.

* * * *

SUDDENLY it is real. Suddenly it is happening. As the occupants of the hotel awake to the crash, his men are in, running upstairs and along corridors, storming the building and making the maximum amount of noise to disorientate the American soldiers as they lie in their beds.

Jagmann is the fourth man in – through the back door, along a narrow corridor and up the stairs. The first floor. In front of him, in the dark, he hears the sound of a boot crashing against wood. A momentary silence as the room is entered and cleared – no-one there.

Other sounds intrude, including the sound of gunfire from the second floor and, at the other end of the corridor, a pistol shot as one of his men stops an American sergeant's attempt to reach for his gun.

Now it is his turn as a light comes on in a room three doors down. First the door. Then, as he looks into the light where five men are in various stages of undress, the grenade. He steps back before rolling it carefully inside, moving another six or seven paces down the corridor to make sure he won't get caught in the blast.

The flash and the noise of the grenade still in his eyes and ears, he turns back to admire his handiwork. Only one man, saved because he has pulled his bed right over on top of him, is alive and moaning. The sounds suggest he will take no further part in this adventure. But to make sure Jagmann fires several times through the bedspread until the moaning stops. For all he knows the American may be feigning pain.

1.25 am. If all is going to plan, every soldier and every naval officer taking part in this raid is in action; within the next five or six minutes the Hotel des Ormes and the old high town of Granville will be theirs.

* * * *

LIEUTENANT Muskie slept on the edge of wakefulness. Over the past eleven months he had trained himself to sleep lightly, not from choice, but from necessity. As soon as he opened his eyes he would be awake, fully awake to the world around him. He had taught himself to catnap, having seen soldiers killed not because they weren't good enough but because they couldn't be soldiers twenty-four hours a day. A soldier who operated with sleep in his eyes, or who couldn't suddenly come to terms with the world, his subconscious always listening for something nasty coming his way, was vulnerable. Death liked nothing better than a man unable to defend himself in the night, as the five men Nikki Jagmann had killed proved with their fumbling hesitancy when he rolled in the grenade, but by 1.22 am, a few seconds after he had first heard the padding footsteps along the corridor, Muskie was up, dressed and moving quietly from his room.

From the balcony above the ballroom and reception area he could see American soldiers, most of them wearing a rich array of underwear or nightwear being escorted at gunpoint down the main stairs to the foyer below. There were about 25 of them, many of them obviously shocked by this attack from nowhere. With their hands on their heads and because of their bizarre attire they looked as if they were playing a very unusual party game.

He couldn't see how many Germans there were; too many to deal with on his own, he guessed, although he was comforted by their battledress. Army men rarely killed in cold blood, unlike the black-uniformed SS, who preferred murder – or, as they usually called it, hiding behind semantics, 'execution'.

Realising the futility of any sort of attack, Lieutenant Muskie made his way to the back of the hotel and eased open one of the first-floor windows, lowering himself down by his fingers from the ledge before dropping as lightly as he could to the yard below.

The fall was no more than seven or eight feet, but the sound, in Muskie's ears, as he landed with a roll and a tumble to the side to lessen the impact, was louder than if he'd jumped from the top. But his luck seemed to hold.

And now? Where now? The Hotel Normandie, he decided. That's where he'd go.

20

High noon after midnight

THE Boulevard des Amiroux was badly named. Although it began in the new town wide and tree-lined, with small cafés on either side, like a scaled-down version of the boulevards in Paris, it narrowed as it came to La Haute Ville, turning from boulevard to road in the space of a dozen yards. Perhaps there had once been fewer houses jostling with each other to hem it in as it wound its way up the hill; perhaps at one time there had been more trees, instead of the few that remained; but for whatever reason it was not attractive by day and was decidedly gloomy by night.

From the point of view of the five soldiers who were now guarding it at the lower end of the road, where it opened up towards the new town, the murky darkness and overhanging French buildings served their purpose well. They had been tucked away in the shadows for nearly half an hour, and although they could only guess how well the attack had been going they were comforted that they had been left alone. Neither friend nor foe had crossed their path, though the sound of incessant gunfire from Le Nec, where the radio control tower had been under attack since the raid began, suggested that the Americans were giving as good as they got. The sound of battle was constant, while the lack of activity, apart from the occasional rapid burst of gunfire from their own soldiers guarding the French barracks, told them that the French soldiers inside had decided discretion was the better part of valour and wouldn't come out to play.

The orders of Heinrich Wolfe and his men, stationed on either side of the road, were simple: they were not to let anyone pass from the old town into the new, or from the new town into the old. Once the raid was over, Jagmann would give them orders to make an orderly retreat. He and they would be the last men to leave the town.

Apart from an initial burst of gunfire a few minutes before, to warn the townspeople to stay inside, they had fired in anger only once; when a butcher living above his boucherie a few yards along the road in the new town had hurried downstairs, turned the light on and opened the door a little to see who was scuffling around outside in the dark.

In many ways it was a relief to Wolfe that the man had appeared. It gave him an excuse to scatter fire into the shop window, killing the light and also killing Henri Le Corre, who slumped back into the house, the door still open, felled by ricocheting bullets. A 59-year-old survivor of the First World War, Monsieur Le Corre had not expected the end would come like this. Without a whimper, without a gesture of defiance, he died.

No lights afterwards, no sound either, as the five men waited in the neck of the road to be told when it was their turn to go. They could, however, see from the rise that lights were being turned on further down the hill, several hundred yards away in the new town; they could even hear a few French voices – none too loud – but still no-one approached or threatened them. No-one, that is, until Muskie crept along the boulevard from the north-east, sliding from doorway to doorway and then stopping, abruptly, as he realised from the sound of the muttered conversation that Wolfe was having with rifleman Schillinger that the way ahead was barred by Germans.

'General-leutnant von Schellenberg's plan seems to be working, Hans,' said Wolfe, in a whisper. 'I wonder if they have found their general yet?'

'Hoffmeister is a good man; if anyone can take the general he can,' replied Hans.

According to their instructions, they would be at their post for at least another forty-five minutes, and they had already decided that as soon as it was time to go they would risk a few precious minutes looking for a French shop to steal food and cigarettes to take back with them to the islands. To do so now would not only be foolhardy – they had been told to defend the street, with their lives if necessary – but foolish as well. You couldn't use a gun effectively if you were weighed down by contraband and it was a foolish soldier who would be killed for the sake of a couple of bottles of wine.

'I wonder how Nikki is getting on at the hotel?' continued Schillinger.

After ten minutes of intense activity in the hotel, which they had heard quite clearly, including at least three explosions as hand grenades were thrown, there had been relatively little noise, apart from the sound of several voices, subdued and unexcited. They had not yet discovered that someone had escaped and was even then stalking them, working out how many Germans there were ahead of him and how best to deal with them.

'He's probably tumbling some pretty French girl even now,' laughed Wolfe. 'He's mad enough to do so'.

Heinrich could not have known it but at that precise moment Nikki was uninterested in any pretty woman and was, instead, ordering his men to search for weapons and to strip the Americans down to their shorts before locking them in the cellar. A quick look inside had told him there were no windows and no way out, apart from the door at the top of the stairs, which could be locked from the other side and then piled high with enough furniture to keep the prisoners trapped for a good hour or so.

Jagmann had given his orders quickly, demanding immediate action, for as soon as possible he wanted to see what was happening at the Hotel Normandie, and how successful Hoffmeister had been in implementing Operation Fahrmann.

Muskie, meanwhile, moved through the gloom, his eyes now accustomed to the dark. He had picked out four men; two together, two on the other side of the road, hiding in shop doorways. The two on his side of the street were in a recess leading into a small shopping arcade. Their guttural speech had alerted him to their presence, and he had already decided to deal with these two first when the sound of a nervous cough warned him that nearer at hand was another man. This one was tucked away in the shadow of a cake shop. The door was open, the man on guard inside, his rifle pointing out to cover the road.

That one would have to be the first to die, Muskie decided, as he crouched as low as he could and, on padded feet, moved stealthily towards the shop's open doorway. And not only would the German have to die, he would also have to die quietly, he told himself, as he saw the outline of a shadowy figure behind the shop counter, his gun not in his hands but lying across the counter pointing out, presumably to give covering fire to the other two men across the road. The men were positioned in such a way that they covered each others' backs, he realised, impressed by the positions they'd taken up but not by their relaxed attitude, as if the job was already done, or unnecessary. If he had been their commanding officer he would have had a few strong words for the two men talking, their words alerting him to their presence and also to this man, whose reason for putting his rifle down was now abundantly clear. He was eating something; bread, perhaps, perhaps a cake, although the shop looked painfully bare of food; and as Muskie crept up, around the counter, and hit him, twice, with the butt of his gun on the back of his neck with as much force as he could muster, it was with something approaching humour that he watched the spray of crumbs spattering across his uniform as the man turned, his piggy eyes dulling over as he slid to the floor. His right arm caught the rifle as he fell, clattering it to the floor.

With bated breath Nick picked up the gun and put it back on the counter, standing, this time, where the man lying on the floor had been thirty seconds before. He coughed, politely; a reasonable copy of the cough he'd heard the man make as he mentally crossed his fingers and hoped his subterfuge would work.

It did. Although a voice called out to him, it didn't seem a question; more a complaint about the noise he was making, and it allowed Mike time to look down at his victim before moving on to despatch Germans two and three.

'It's a wonder he didn't choke to death,' he thought, abstractedly, as he climbed over the German's body and back out into the midnight air, the enemy rifle remaining as as he'd placed it, pointing out along the counter. The German, meanwhile, all thoughts of war lost in some deep, deep sleep, looked a peculiar sight, his helmet askew and his mouth and cheeks puffed out with cake.

'Where to now, Michael?' Muskie said under his breath, knowing that collaring this first soldier had been a lucky break and that if the other men had been doing their job properly they would have realised something was wrong. Time now to be a professional soldier. He decided that he would have to take the next two men out together if he could, before using his knowledge of the back streets and alleyways to make his escape.

He eased himself out into the street again, daring himself to pass the four remaining guards and to get to the Hotel Normandie as quickly as possible. He knew he could edge his way close to the men this side of the street before they would see him, and he guessed that they had been told not to leave their post if anyone squeezed by. Well, if that was the case, he would see how obedient they were to their commanding officer and, if they were stupid enough to follow him they would quickly find that they were fighting in his territory and on his terms, not theirs.

High on adrenaline and very clear in his mind about the next move to make, he took a deep breath, and with a disarming smile and with the air of someone lost and needing to ask the way he came out of hiding.

'Hi there fellows,' he said, his voice pleasantly matter-of-fact for the time of night. 'You guys enjoying the party?'

He couldn't get a clear shot at either from where he'd been hiding but he could if he was level with them. So, having filled the air with this late night pleasantry, he threw himself down, rolled on the pavement and shot into the arcade from the gutter.

The Germans, startled first by his voice and then by the gunfire, were slow to respond. The two men across the street were slightly quicker, but not quick enough to fire accurately at this tall American who had breached their blockade, had picked himself up and was now running past them, making long, easy strides as he ran away from La Haute Ville. A burst of gunfire followed, but he was already twenty yards past and slowing down to turn a corner. The noise of a machine-gun rattling in the night seemed impossibly loud in the narrow street, hemmed in by old houses, and for a moment or two it deafened Muskie, who had stopped and was hugging the wall, waiting for the gunfire to stop. What, he wondered, would the Germans do next? Would they follow him? And should he alter his plans to try to phone for help?

The decision was made for him as another man appeared; this one from the same direction he'd just come from – the Hotel des Ormes.

He was obviously a German officer, he realised as he looked back, for the men were full of apologies and his angry tone left them in no doubt that he was extremely displeased that a lone American had managed to sneak past as if they hadn't been there. Although Muskie couldn't speak a word of German, the tone of the officer's barked commands, which he could hear quite clearly, brought a smile to his lips. He could imagine exactly what was being said.

The conversation, such as it was, lasted no more than a few seconds before two of the guards – one from each side of the road – followed apprehensively down the road. Without doubt they had been ordered to seek him out and kill him. Two against one; and with the odd sensation that this was some kind of re-run of a Gary Cooper movie, Lieutenant Muskie checked his gun before moving on. Behind him the Germans were covering each other as they darted from pillar to post, more frightened of him, perhaps, than he would ever be of them.

As the sound of his footsteps echoed in the street one of them fired, blindly at the place where Muskie had been fifteen seconds before. The bullets rat-a-tat-tatted across the cobbles, bouncing against dustbins and peppering into the ¾-inch plywood boarding up a shoeshop. Muskie, however, was already further up the side street, knowing exactly where he would go. As the other German soldier also opened fire, the bullets stitching a line from one side of the road to the other, he crashed through into a darkened alleyway where three dustbins, stuffed full of ashes and papers, were stacked against a wall. He overturned the first one he came to, and kicked it back, along the cobblestones, before throwing himself onwards and out into a small overgrown garden. This, in turn, led to another alleyway, which opened out into the same street but twenty yards further back, behind the Germans. As he poked his head around the alleyway he was amused to find that one of the two men, perhaps in terror, had thrown a grenade at the bin and that both men were peppering the spot where it had been with a generous helping of bullets. Twisted metal and a few pieces of burning paper had become their target, and the enthusiastic way they were opening fire suggested they were hoping against hope that somewhere in the débris they'd find their man.

Well, they hadn't found him and the diversion had given Muskie the upper hand.

As he tracked their every move the blaze from burning papers illuminated them nicely as they crouched low in shop doorways, waiting nervously for any movement from the American soldier. They still believed he was in front of them, and that they were protected. But he wasn't – he was behind.

'Hi, Fritz,' sang Muskie, taking careful aim, and as a German half-turned, a look of horror etched in his face, Muskie fired.

The bullet tore through the man's side. Another bullet tore through his arm, and, with an astonished look in his eyes as he tried to work out where this tall American had come from, Heinrich Wolfe fell to the floor, not dead, but dying. All thoughts of war, all thoughts of attempting to return fire had completely left his mind.

With the clinical detachment of a professional soldier knowing that he has one enemy fewer to deal with Muskie focused his attention on the other man. Without pausing to admire his handiwork, and in one fluid movement he stepped across to his left before taking careful aim.

The other soldier, however, had had enough; and the American Lieutenant was first amused, and then flattered, by the speed with which the other yelped, threw down his gun as if it was blistering his hands and ran away down the Rue Militaire, screaming into the night.

'War plays funny tricks on a man,' thought Muskie, as he moved back into the safety of the roadside shadows, listening in case the third man, the leader, might also be following. After a while, hearing only the crackle of the paper burning, and the rasping breath of the German soldier dying, he ventured out back into the street. There was no-one there.

Deciding that he would find a phone somewhere to call for reinforcements, the Lieutenant's next priority was the powerful MG-34 Mauser lying in the street close to the body of the man he'd just shot. It was ugly-looking and far too heavy for this kind of street battle, but it had the capacity to kill more people much more quickly than his own Colt .45.

Once he had the gun, and once he'd awoken up the mayor to insist he telephoned through to Cherbourg HQ, he would tiptoe his way back to the Hotel Normandie to make as much mischief as possible to spoil this raid. He couldn't defeat the German army single-handed, but he could amuse himself by picking off the officers, one by one, damaging their pride and making them feel very sorry they'd sacrificed a good night's sleep to visit Granville. For a brief moment he relaxed, leaving the shadows that had been protecting him and savouring the cool night air.

But as he bent down to pick up the dead German's gun he heard it: the sound of a footstep, soft indeed, but not soft enough to be disguised as anything other than a footfall. It was about fifteen yards behind him.

'Hello, Fritz,' he said, damning himself for not realising that this was the guarded approach of a professional, before throwing himself from the street to the same doorway the soldier he'd killed had been hiding in.

'Thank the lord,' Muskie thought to himself, 'that the fire in front of me's gone out . . .'

He was the professional soldier again; and although he would have preferred the German rifle, he was not prepared to reach through the shadows to get it. Like his unknown enemy, he remained silent. He would have to readjust if he was to deal with this other man and he realised, not without some desperation, that he was at a distinct disadvantage. He had shown his hand – this other man knew where he was and knew how good he was; and Fritz no. 2 was stalking him properly, biding his time until the right moment to kill.

What was equally as galling to the American was that he couldn't see through the shadows to where the other man might be. The other man, somewhere out there in the dark, knew where he was and what he was up against. 'Knowledge enormous makes a god of me,' he remembered in a vague kind of way; but that knowledge no longer lay with him, but the enemy.

The Rue Militaire was now silent, as it had been for several minutes, and to all intents and purposes the street was no longer the scene of battle. Then, just as Muskie was just debating with himself whether to leap out into the night again, some foolhardy soul turned an upstairs bedroom light on fifteen yards away. The curtains of the room had been drawn tight, but they were thin and fitted badly, and the light filtering through the glass was nearly enough to reveal Muskie, who was holding himself as close as he could into the narrow doorway, ready to spring. 'Christ,' he thought frantically, trying to work out how to deal with this new state of affairs, and to turn defence into attack. 'Haven't I enough problems already without some damn fool trying to light me up like I'm the star of the screen?'

As calmly as he could, although he noticed that for the first time in nearly eleven months his hand was shaking, he searched in his pocket for his old brass lighter. He found it, held it as far away as possible with his left hand and struck the flint, creating a sudden blaze of fire. This he threw out into the road up the hill behind him and darted forwards, low, from this doorway to another, as a grenade landed in the doorway where he'd been hiding and blew out the door and the window in a blast of white light.

The sound of the explosion was deafening in such a confined space and Mike could only guess the effect it had had on the people living there. 'The guy's playing this for keeps,' he thought, admiring the logic of using a grenade. No pussyfooting around with guns and bullets.

The direction of the throw had told him where the German was hiding; to his left, on the opposite side of the road, nearer to him than he had imagined.

Muskie was a much happier man as he looked along the barrel of his gun, aiming it midway between the bomb-damaged house and the narrow archway from where the grenade had been thrown. The initiative was all his now and he could imagine the indecision in the German's mind. Should he come out into the street to see if the grenade had blown the American into tiny bits and pieces? Should he stay where he was, or perhaps do as the American had done, and dart from one doorway to another, tempting his enemy to open fire?

Lieutenant Muskie didn't know which option his enemy would take, but he allowed himself a wry smile at his opponent's dilemma. Uncertainty was the key to defeating an enemy in a dog-fight such as this. Give a live soldier a sense of uncertainty and within a couple of minutes the uncertainty would be over – he'd be dead. You could bet on it.

Then, in the worst possible way, the battle turned. Someone inside the house behind him turned a light on. Not an upstairs light but a hallway light, illuminating the small archway above the main front door. It was a dirty little apology of a window, no more than the size of half a large dinner-plate, but it allowed enough light to escape to show his unprotected right side, enough light to allow Nikki Jagmann time to take aim and fire.

The first bullet, when it came, hit Mike Muskie's right arm an inch above the elbow.

'Too fast. It's all happening too fast,' he realised, frantically.

The next bullets, when they came, tore into both legs, below the knee. 'Too fast! Too fast! It's all happening too fast!' he cried aloud. 'I need more time!'

And then, coming to terms with the pain and trying desperately to take aim with both hands on the gun, as his shattered right arm refused to respond, he saw him: his enemy. A good looking man, powerfully built, but with slim hips and an angular body, a man not unlike himself, even to the extent that he was taking deliberate aim; first at the stomach, then the head.

Jagmann knew that the trembling hands of the injured man in front of him didn't have the power to pull the trigger, knew, as he had seen so many times before, that this was simply another soldier with the mark of death already on his face. With a half smile on his face began to pull the trigger of his own gun.

'Michelle!'

The cry came from behind the injured American.

Not content to turn the light on in the hall, some idiot French peasant woman had decided to open the hallway door, the light tumbling out into the shadows of night. Her husband, unshaven and only partly dressed, was bellowing out to her to stay inside. 'Merde. Let these fools kill each other if they wish, but don't get involved.'

It was enough. The German, for some reason paused, lowered his gun slightly and peered into the light of the doorway behind as Michelle Le Vesconte gasped at the two men, barely ten yards apart, with one of them seemingly close to death, his arm and legs a mass of blood. A man's hand snaked around the door and pulled her back inside, roughly.

'You little fool, do you want to get killed?'

Aiming with the right hand but pulling the trigger with his left Muskie shot, not once, but twice.

The battle of Rue Militaire was over: the American had won.

21

Silk pyjamas

MAJOR Thomas Farthing folded his clothes neatly, as was his custom, and placed them on a chair by the door. It was a pleasant enough room, and the luxury of a double bed and privacy were something he had not enjoyed since leaving New York six months before, where he'd said goodbye to his wife and young son. His thoughts were often of home, where he had begun to make a name for himself as a hard-working administrator in New York, Boston and Washington, where his talents were much appreciated by the military hierarchy. It had been he who had volunteered for this trip to Europe, although he knew that it would be hard and, by all accounts, a thankless task to help restore order and efficiency to Europe. He also knew that once he was in the war proper he would have to give up certain luxuries, and it had been a careful Major Farthing who had packed his clothes in his suitcase to come to Europe to help administer the wreck of a broken continent. Perhaps the greatest luxury of all were the silk pyjamas he had brought with him. They were a present from his wife which, as yet, he had not dared to wear in the close confines of dormitory rooms where he had been sleeping alongside fellow officers. Now, however, for the first time, safe behind Allied lines, in a four-star hotel and anticipating the luxury of a double bed, he would strip, wash, clad himself in silk and fall happily asleep.

This had been the theory – although the truth was a little less pleasing; for as he undressed and made ready for bed there remained in his mouth a sour taste, which came from talking to that soft-spoken lieutenant, Muskie. He might have been a good ten years younger, but in looks and attitude Muskie seemed a product of a much harder generation. He had also shown scant regard for seniority, which surprised Farthing, not least because he had made every effort to get on with such a diffident young man. The sour taste was still there as he climbed into bed, and he was in half a mind to talk to his senior officer, Colonel Anderson, the next day about respect for rank, and the importance of discipline, as he attempted to make himself comfortable between the starched white sheets. This in itself was not an easy task. The mattress was too soft and what passed for a pillow was too hard. This was a hideous, typically French bolster, which couldn't be softened no matter how hard you hit it, so it was a good few minutes before Major Farthing found a niche for himself which was less uncomfortable than all the rest.

As he lay on his back, having discarded completely the overstuffed pillow, his eyes looked up at the ceiling and, in a stream of consciousness that began with Lieutenant Muskie and ended in his bedroom, he relived the feeling that somewhere, two or three floors above, something nasty had happened not so very long ago. What it might have been he didn't know; but he would find out tomorrow. At times like these he cursed the powers of a good imagination.

It was just before midnight when Major Farthing fell asleep; a blissful sleep, which would have continued for another seven or eight hours if he hadn't been woken up at around 1.30 am in the most unexpected of ways.

The door was kicked open – no lights outside apart from a faint glimmer from somewhere further down the corridor – and there, framed in the doorway stood the shadowy figure of a burly German in full battledress, huge by comparison with the door frame, a grey shape nestling a small, stub-nosed submachine gun to his chest.

'Out, please. Downstairs, please.'

Three words carefully learnt, although it was the gun which was doing most of the talking.

Major Farthing looked at it, and then again at the German soldier. It must, he decided, be a trick; and he was not going to fall for it.

'How dare you! Invading someone's bedroom at this time of the night. Do you know what time it is? And do you know who you're talking to?'

But it was a pointless tirade. Eduard Nolte, behind the gun, had only twelve or thirteen English words at his command and he'd already used up three of them.

'Downstairs please. Downstairs. I kill you.'

The slight tightening on the trigger made Major Farthing realise that this German soldier wasn't part of some elaborate game, and having pulled on a jacket over his pyjamas (despite the German's insistence that he went as he was) and with boots in hand, he was bundled downstairs with the minimum of fuss on the German's part but, whining and complaining every step of the way, with the maximum amount of fuss on his.

It was only when he was pushed blinking into the harsh light of the main room where he had chatted with his fellow officers a few hours before that he realised he was not the only one to suffer such a gross indignity, and that this burly German soldier wasn't acting alone. Here were more German commandos; some with blackened faces through which their eyes gleamed like pale blue slits. They were obviously in complete control of the hotel as they herded together the remaining residents, all UNRRA people with the exception of four or five soldiers whose job had been to protect them in the event of raids such as this. If he had been more fully aware of the number of Germans who'd taken part he could have had some sympathy with the unhappy GIs, but his main emotion was still one of anger that anyone should dare destroy the sanctity of sleep.

At a glance he weighed up the situation. Eighteen prisoners, including the five soldiers who had been disarmed, and who'd been ordered to take off their boots to prevent them running away. Another twelve, like himself, half-dressed or in sleeping attire, as other 'guests' were hurried downstairs to join them.

'You had better put on your boots, Major,' said one of the men, older than the rest and seemingly in complete control. Relaxed, as he perched on the edge of a desk, he looked the silk pyjamaed American up and down with an amused eye.

But no. Major Farthing decided that he would not co-operate until this bullying German officer knew that he would not tolerate such brutish behaviour.

'This . . . this is an outrage. I am an administrator, not a fighting soldier. I insist that you leave this hotel immediately. You have already lost the war and anything you do to us will . . .'

'Waste of time, Major,' said Colonel Anderson, drily. 'That big guy won't take no for an answer. Still, if you want to be a hero, just edge away from the rest of us if you would, please. Bullets have a tendency to kind of ricochet around. If you know what I mean.'

The Colonel made a point of moving away, closer to the other prisoners who were watching this charade, afraid but curious as to how this German-American confrontation would end. The other man, the German, without appearing to move closer to Major Farthing, somehow seemed to grow in size, to become bulkier, heavier, as he leant further no more than an inch or two and said, in an undertone, full of hidden menace: 'And where is the General? Where is your Commandant, Herr Eisenhower?'

The sound of firing in a street nearby and a loud explosion very close on the pierhead made the Major start. There were other Germans here, he realised, peevishly, and they were blowing up the town. But why? And why on earth should these strange men imagine that Eisenhower was here, when it had been several weeks since he'd packed his bags and returned to the front?

The realisation that they might not believe him when he told them that General Eisenhower had flown the coop, that they might become terribly angry, made him more nervous than at any time since his sleep had been so discourteously disturbed.

And as he realised the true meaning of the explosions outside – that this was the business end of war – he discovered something inside himself he hadn't fully realised until now; that he didn't want to be a hero, and that he didn't want to die. A thin film of sweat began to bead his brow, and Major Thomas James Farthing tried desperately hard to look away from those hooded eyes of the German officer, who was looking at him, half-smiling, awaiting a reply. If it were the wrong reply, the good Major realised with fast-growing panic, all the bluster in the world wouldn't save him, nor the authority of his neat clean uniform, most of it still hanging on a peg in his upstairs room.

It was Colonel Anderson who broke the silence.

'I've told him once, Major, that Ike's halfway to Berlin but he won't believe me. Seems he won't go home until he's got himself a general.'

'It's true,' said the Major, casting a thankful glance in the Colonel's direction. 'It's true. Believe me. Find out from your own men. He's no longer here, hasn't been for weeks. Why, if he was, would the hotel be so open to attack?' From the loud complaint of a moment ago, the Major's tone had changed to a whine.

Hoffmeister looked down at this silk-clad major in front of him, with his top-quality leather boots and jacket. He had half a mind to believe him. But he had to be sure.

A sudden thought that this man, with the wispy ginger hair drawn across his head might be Eisenhower flashed across his mind, but no, he had studied his photographs and had read the reports too many times. He had learned his looks too well to believe that this could possibly be *the* general.

'In which room was he sleeping, please?' asked Hoffmeister, as if he were the hotel manager, worried that his staff weren't properly catering for the comforts of his guest.

'The one I was in was – room 24 on the first – no second floor,' stuttered the Major, all the fizz gone out of him.

The tone confirmed that this was no battle-hardened general. He seemed too afraid to lie – but Hoffmeister had to make sure. Taking what appeared to be the largest hand-gun Farthing had ever seen from the holster on his belt, and pointing it directly at the Major's head, Colonel Hoffmeister asked again, only a little bit louder.

'Please; before I shoot, to tell the truth.'

'He's not here; he's gone to join the others, to make certain he's one of the first ones in when they take Berlin. Please. You must believe me. I wouldn't lie!'

Eyes wide open and with legs suddenly unable to bear his weight, Major Farthing truly believed he was about to die.

Even Colonel Anderson felt sorry for this half-clad administrator, who had come to Europe believing the only live German soldiers he would meet would be prisoners-of-war. He looked at his white knuckles, as he clung on tightly to the back of a chair for support. If the German said 'boo' loudly enough the other man would probably die of fright. He wondered uneasily how close they all were to death. The German looked hard enough and callous enough to pull the trigger, but you could never be sure. As a betting man he'd give odds of two to one that within an hour Farthing would be dead – odds that Farthing was trying desperately hard to readjust in his favour.

'I'm telling the truth. You must believe me.' Fewer than forty-eight hours on French soil and he was about to be executed by a German officer, when he'd been assured there wasn't an enemy division within a two hundred-mile radius!

Another soldier said something, the one who had brought him down from his room, and after a few terse words in German and a momentary hesitation the big officer lowered the gun a fraction, and smiled.

'He says you cannot be a high ranking general and that your uniform is too new for you to be an important man. You can thank Private Dorf for your life.'

Acknowledging this, and conscious that there would have been more armed soldiers present within the Hotel Normandie if Eisenhower had been staying here, Hoffmeister relaxed his grip and returned the gun to its black leather holster. As he did so Farthing visibly folded.

His ordeal though was far from over. For Hoffmeister's instructions had made it quite clear that he was to take back with him to Jersey a general; and although this man was not a man of presence, and was only a major, he was a man of some authority – his uniform and silk pyjamas told him that. He would have to do.

'All the officers and the men given the best hotel rooms,' Hoffmeister said, with some urgency, to Jacob Kesselring. 'Take their papers, give them shoes or slippers and escort them to the beach.'

He clicked his fingers, impatient to be away, and gave Farthing a smile of quite malicious enjoyment.

'A poor substitute for a general,' he said, in English, looking him up and down and noticing for the first time how over-nourished he was, compared with his own hungry men. 'But the Befehlshaber will make you most welcome.'

As he gave rapid instructions to his men to take the prisoners to their ships, ever conscious of the time fast ticking away, he couldn't help but feel a little sad, realising, with a fading heart, that if Eisenhower were on his way to Berlin then within a few weeks the war really would be over. What chance had Germany now? And what had this little excursion gained, but to serve as a tiny pin-prick in the Allied side, to remind them of the 26,000 soldiers still hemmed in within the islands? But, ever the realist, he remained grateful for being given the chance to fight; and if they didn't have a top class hostage at least they had several prisoners who might be worth something to them in any future negotiations.

He turned to his men. All the rooms, Kesselring told him, had been searched. A glace at his watch showed that they had fifteen minutes left before the deadline – fifteen minutes before the hotel would explode in a riot of flame and fire, and enough time for one last look around the hotel restaurant.

As Major Farthing, Colonel Anderson and another half dozen prisoners were bundled out into the night, and having cast a quick glance at the two sacks crammed full of documents to be taken to the boats, Hoffmeister ordered a complete evacuation of the hotel before wrenching one of the large cupboard doors open in the restaurant itself. Knives, forks, table linen – but no wine. He shrugged his shoulders, glanced at his watch, and walked quickly through the imposing double doors of the Hotel Normandie, back towards the Boulevard des Amiroux, but not so quickly that he couldn't savour the satisfaction of a job well done. For the first time in over eighteen months he had re-entered the war, as he was paid to do, as a soldier. And although the Granville raid would not end the war, there was no doubt that for this night at least the Germans had regained a small part of France and a great deal of pride. If only the rest of their battered Ninth Army, fighting valiantly under General Wenck near Schwiechlow Lake, could do the same.

Hoffmeister quickened his pace away from the hotel, the last man down the steps, and hurried around the corner where the remaining two guards told him of the fighting that had taken place when an American had broken out of the old town, to be tracked by Wolfe and Steinbach, and that they, and their commanding officer, Jagmann, had not been seen again.

True, they had heard a great deal of noise – mainly gunfire, and the last two shots had only been heard a minute or two before – but they had been told to stay where they where to defend the road, and neither was prepared to disobey orders and take the initiative.

From their tone of voice Hoffmeister guessed that they would have been none too keen to leave their posts to find out what had happened to the smart American, but it was pointless to order them to find out now. Instead he ordered them back to the ships and would have followed, too, if Lieutenant Jagmann hadn't been his friend. He felt it was his duty to Nikki and to his wife, Katrin, to spend a final few minutes on French soil finding out exactly what had happened.

22

Fare thee well

KNOWING that he had at the most five minutes to find Jagmann, Hoffmeister strode quickly towards the Rue Militaire, scene of the most recent Granville street battle. He was one of the few Germans left within the confines of the town. The others were Otto von Bastion, killed during the abortive raid on the radar station at Le Nec, Walther Klugmann, who was slumped beneath the bakery shop counter with a mouth full of cake and a fractured skull, and the two soldiers Muskie had dealt with in his street battle. One of these was dead, the other hiding, too frightened to return along the cobblestone street and too ashamed to find another way back to the boats. All the other officers and men had returned to harbour. Some were already back on board the minesweepers standing by in the port; others were clambering into one of the two boats standing ready to ferry them out to their mother ships. One boat was ready to leave; the other would leave at ten minutes to three.

As Hoffmeister turned the corner into the Rue Militaire, keeping as close to the wall as he could, flattening himself into the shadows, he feared the worst – not for himself but for Nikki Jagmann, too good a friend, too good a soldier to be left behind. Hoffmeister had good reason to be worried for Nikki's safety; for if he had intended catching the last boat out of the harbour he would already be at the quayside, laughing and joking with the rest of his men, and he knew that although his friend took risks they were always calculated risks. He wouldn't want to be a hero if it meant being stranded here, in this messy little French town.

The Rue Militaire was quiet now, no-one daring to open another door in case they, too, should perish by bullet or bomb. The only sound was the occasional booming of the German guns out at sea; guns fired as a reminder to the townspeople to stay indoors as Operation Fahrmann came to an end.

Gun in hand, Hoffmeister entered the road, taking note of the cobbles, of the dirt and, as his eyes got used to the darkness, of the shadows where a man lay, motionless, in the middle of the street.

He was dead. Even from where he stood, at the corner, he could sense the stiffness of death. But the other man, there, about twenty yards away, cursing under his breath while trying to staunch the bleeding from his left leg with a tourniquet fashioned from the ripped sleeve of his jacket, wasn't.

Only one light illuminated the scene, all other lights had been extinguished as rapidly as the instant it had taken Lieutenant Muskie to fire two shots into Jagmann's belly and head.

Treading cautiously towards where the first man had fallen, conscious that this could well be a trap, Colonel Hoffmeister was three or four strides away when he realised that his worst fears had been realised. This bloody face, half-blown away, had once attracted women with its smile and mocking eyes. Now the eyes were misted over, bulging, sightless, and the smile had been replaced by a thick wedge of blood. The gun lying a yard away was no use to him now. Nikki Jagmann, good soldier, firm friend, was dead. No more women to lust after, no more wives, their daughters fast asleep in another bedroom, to give his sexual favours to; just a hunk of dead meat lying in a grimy street in a poky little French seaside town.

'Help me. Can you help me, please?'

It was the other man, the man who had killed his friend who was speaking.

Curious, but no longer alarmed, Hoffmeister walked past Nikki, and towards the American.

'You there. Can you help me?' said Muskie, busy trying to stop the bleeding from his shattered legs.

'My legs . . .'

'And him,' said Hoffmeister in his best English. 'How did he die?'

The American, too interested in his own wounds to be concerned with the body of the German soldier, was dismissive in his reply.

'Him. He's dead. It was him or me. Hasn't moved for a good five minutes . . .'

The response of the large man in front of him was not quite what Lieutenant Muskie had wanted, and it took a few seconds to realise, through eyes misted with pain and sweat, that the voice had belonged not as he had at first imagined to one of the good guys, but to the baddies – an enemy who was currently pointing a large handgun directly at his chest. In the most polite, most formal of tones Hoffmeister said: 'Nikki Jagmann was a good man; a good soldier.' He tightened his finger a little on the trigger. 'He did not deserve to die. He has a wife and two children. They will be grieved by his death.'

If it unnerved the American it didn't show. And, as Hoffmeister realised afterwards, it was the casualness of the man that had changed his mind, a casualness which made him decide not to shoot.

In terrible pain from his wounds and losing blood rapidly, Muskie didn't say a word. He just shrugged his shoulders and carried on tightening the tourniquet he'd fashioned from the sleeve of his jacket as blood continued to trickle down his legs, where it congealed in a small pool beneath his army issue black boots. He had lost all interest in either his executioner, or his gun, which was on the cobbles in front of him.

Hoffmeister picked up the weapon as a keepsake, turned and walked rapidly back down the hill, towards the boats.

'Ah for a breath of good German air,' he thought, as he passed the window of a scruffy French bar, one or two bottles of very cheap red wine on display inside. 'Not even Calvados.

But ah, I will drink to you tonight, Nikki Jagmann, and wish you the choicest women in heaven.' As he murmured this, he used the American's gun to smash the window. He then grabbed a bottle by the neck and, having zipped it up inside his thick leather jacket, ran down the hill. 'Goodbye American!' he shouted and then, as an afterthought, in his own language, 'Treat my countrymen with kindness when you enter Berlin!'

With that he was away past the houses and onto the beach, back out to sea, in the last boat, a minute to spare before Klugmann would have ordered the ships home without him.

Back home; back to the sparse existence on the fortress island.

* * * *

GENERAL von Schellenberg learnt about the mixed success of the raid two days later. The credit – for the action was seen as a victory by the German hierarchy in Berlin – was all Hoffmeister's, he was told. The ignominy of having to leave behind a perfectly sound minesweeper in the mud didn't seem to matter. Five ships captured, two with crew, one American gunboat claimed as sunk and eleven relatively important prisoners taken all contributed to the success. The remainder of the picture was acceptable, too. True, there were five missing, including Jagmann, all presumed dead, but the assault force left a ruined harbour, which had been effectively put out of action for several weeks at least, and one large hotel destroyed by a soldier who proved himself much more efficient than the Boy, Thomas Schmidt. And, von Schellenberg had noted with quiet satisfaction, when the hotel had been blown it fell in upon itself with no loss of German life. He knew this because he had been shown the wire; for in this moment of triumph Kreiser had not forgotten him, and in one of the several dispatches he had sent direct to the Berlin bunker where Hitler seemed to be spending all of his time these days, he had mentioned, tersely, that some of the credit undoubtedly belonged to the former island Kommandant, Pieter von Schellenberg.

But the letter of praise, though well-intentioned, meant nothing to him now. Nothing could save him from the 'justice' meted out by the Gestapo. For tacitly agreeing that the plot to kill Hitler was a good one – he had, after all, known about it but had not alerted any of Hitler's staff that it was about to happen – Baron von Schellenberg, sixth generation general, whose grandfather had served under the chancellorship of Bismarck, had been given two choices. First, the full ignominy of a public trial and humiliation, almost certainly to be followed by death and the seizure of all his goods and chattels, which would mean that Marte, his wife, who had been released and was back in their Schloss in Lotz, would inherit nothing. Second a much quicker end . . . this, by his own hand.

In this bare room, with his service revolver lying on the table, he knew he had made the right choice; although he was saddened that he would never see his son or beloved Marte again.

At the same time he wouldn't miss the Germany that would come after the little Austrian corporal, the house painter, had been toppled from power. It would, he knew, be a very different Fatherland to the one he had known. It would be humiliated, beaten, and with enemies enough to bleed the country dry.

The last words of the Gestapo officer – on the surface such a nice man, simply doing a job – were the last words he would ever hear, as he placed the gun barrel in his mouth and slowly pulled back the trigger.

'You should not have told all of your secrets to your father confessor,' was what the man had said. 'For be sure your sins will find you out . . . '

Endpiece

ON 9 March, 1945, the very day that US troops captured intact the bridge over the Rhine at Remagen, an assault force sent from the Channel Islands did, indeed, take prisoner the seaside town of Granville, on the Cotentin peninsula, for about three hours. It was a raid that General-leutnant Graf von Schmettow, commander of the 319 Division and Commander-in-chief of the Channel Islands had been planning since early February, 1945, when the first raid on Granville had been launched – a raid that was abandoned when a choppy sea made it difficult to transfer assault troops to Hafenschutz landing boats. But the fact that his force had sailed within twenty yards of the small French harbour undetected proved to von Schmettow that such a raid could succeed with the right tidal conditions and under a pitch black sky.

Von Schmettow, and later his chief of staff, Vice-admiral Friedrich Huffmeier, planned a second attack. It was to be larger and, if anything, more scrupulously organised than the first, and its aim was to bring back coal ships, to destroy the fortifications of the town, and to capture as many important officers as they could find stationed there.

There was vague talk of stealing a general – General Eisenhower – who had made his base five miles to the south of Granville the previous September. By the time of the raid, however, he had long gone, although no-one was too sure which army officers might be tucked up in bed in the Normandie Hotel, cosily asleep in the belief that they were 300 miles from the nearest enemy threat.

At around 1 am on 9 March their dreams were rudely shattered as German commandos stormed the hotel and the town. To this day you can see the scars of battle, in the form of bullet holes above a butcher's shop.

For over two hours the old town of Granville was occupied and controlled by the German raiding party. But they didn't control all of the town; the radar station, for example, wasn't taken and Leutnant zur Zee Scheufele, leader of the assault party detailed to destroy it, was killed by American troops who had rallied to its defence. The Normandie Hotel, on the other hand, was easily taken; the self-same hotel which earlier in the war had been used by the Gestapo for interrogation purposes. Sadly, the meathooks on the wall and the bloodstains on the floor aren't an invention.

Among the prisoners of war the Germans took with them to the Channel Islands were five American servicemen and John Alexander, BSc, a mild-mannered welfare officer, and the only member of the United Nations Relief and Rehabilitation Administration (UNRRA) to be captured by the enemy. They also took with them sixty-seven of their own prisoners of war, German soldiers who had been captured by the Allies and put to work in the docks at Granville, where they unloaded coal from British colliers.

Meanwhile, as German commandos took charge of the streets and harbour, one minesweeper, the M412, found itself in difficulty. It had become stuck in the sand and stayed there, forcing her captain to swap his expensive, fully-armed minesweeper for a dumpy little collier.

By 3 am the raid was over. Three Germans had been killed, fifteen wounded, and one was missing. He was later picked up by the Americans. For the Allies the losses were substantially higher. One American army officer, eight British seamen and six French civilians were killed, while on the ill-fated PC 564 which did indeed take on three mighty German gunships, fourteen men were killed, eleven wounded and fourteen 'lost at sea', although it was later discovered that they had been rescued by the Germans, who added them to their hostage list and brought them back to Jersey, where they had to suffer along with the rest of the island the privations of war. Food was scarce, and despite the success of the Granville raid, the occupying forces were under no illusion that they were losing the war. If they ever did try to delude themselves that this was not the case, the islanders were quick to tell them otherwise. Although the Germans had banned radio sets they couldn't find and destroy them all. By the end of the Occupation the islanders had a much better idea of what was happening in the wider world than any ordinary German soldier.

This is all true of the wartime situation in the Channel Islands. The truth, however, is very different from this book, which is largely a lie. The feud between von Schmettow and Huffmeier, for example, the army commander versus the ambitious naval would-be-Befehlshaber, was not as I have portrayed it, and their characters and looks were very different in real life. Von Schellenberg and Kreiser are the products of imagination but also of the fact that by February, 1945, the real people – von Schmettow and Huffmeier – weren't on speaking terms. As long ago as 17 October, 1944, a fellow German officer scribbled on a report from Huffmeier: 'They don't even speak to each other now!' Similarly, when von Schmettow left the islands it was because Huffmeier had helped to ease him out of his job. A telegram telling the island Kommandant he was going is also proof that he was mistrusted by High Command, partly because he was suspected of having been involved in the failed attempt to kill Hitler the previous July. Dated 27 February, 1945, it reads: 'C-in-C West Naval Chief Command West: 319 Infantry Division.

'With immediate effect General Graf von Schmettow, commander of the 319th Infantry Division and Commander-in-chief of the Channel Islands is transferred for health reasons to the supreme command of the Army's officers pool and Vice-admiral Huffmeier, Sea Defence Commandant and Chief of Staff, Channel Islands, is appointed Commander-in-chief, Channel Islands. A new commander for the 319th Infantry Division will be ordered by personnel division. Lt-General Graf von Schmettow is to be dispatched at once, without awaiting the arrival of the new divisional commander.'

If it had been in his power Huffmeier would have defended the islands to the bitter end, but thankfully for the islanders, when the German High Command surrendered on 7 May there was little point in carrying on the war purely for the sake of military glory. Huffmeier surrendered, and was denied the opportunity of adding Oak leaves to his Knight's Cross, which he had won earlier in the war before being transferred to the islands.

Two days before the German High Command capitulated, on 5 May, 1945, General Eisenhower himself gave his blessing to the liberation of the Channel Islands, or Operation Nestegg as it was known, and at 10.45 am, 12 May, Huffmeier formally surrendered to Brigadier A E Snow.

Meanwhile, what of von Schmettow? Was he truly faced with the choice of death or dishonour? Thankfully, no – although for several weeks he was a worried man. He survived, and eventually returned to the islands as a private citizen, over twenty years after he had first served there as Befehlshaber der Kanalinseln – Commander-in-chief, Channel Islands.

But never forget that this is fiction. The characters are imaginary and the 'facts' have been sufficiently manipulated to provide the kind of semi-true adventure an author needs to tell a story. So although Nikki Jagmann might have been a huge womaniser, always living life on the edge, only the author knows his real name and in which age he truly lived. And although Mike Muskie might have been based in Granville, kicking his heels until something more promising came along, the chances are that his creation is a complete fabrication, a chance encounter between the need for an American hero and the author's word processor.

Finally, if anyone is interested enough to look deeper, beneath the fiction to the fact below, they could do no better than read Michael Ginns' excellent account entitled 'The Granville Raid' in After the Battle, No 47 (London, 1985). Other publications used to help tell the story include 'The Missing Link – USS PC 564' by Margaret Ginns, from the Channel Islands Occupation Review series (Jersey), 'Islands in Danger' by Alan and Mary Seaton Wood, New English Library (London, 1965) and 'The German Occupation of the Channel Islands' by Dr Charles Cruickshank, Alan Sutton (Stroud, 1990). All these books tell the history, unlike 'Islands at War', which is meant to be an adventure story taking no sides as it reveals the thoughts and actions of a few characters who *might* have lived during World War II.

In the book the main characters are judged not in terms of their race or political beliefs, but as people; so Mike Muskie and Nikki Jagmann, though a continent apart, are really the same kind of man, who would both acknowledge in each other the same animal qualities that come to the surface in times of war. War brings out the hunter in them and both are excellent hunters. Only Willie Hoffmeister would have been a better hunter, because he would never have taken unnecessary risks. Note, for example, that he hadn't actually gone into the Emerald Hotel the night it exploded; and in France he ordered his soldiers to take the Normandie Hotel while he waited outside, timing them, before joining them six minutes later. In real life Hoffmeister would have emerged from the war comparatively unscathed. It was a job to him, something he had to do, and if he had to do it, he might as well do it well. He had no time for fanatics, like Kreiser, and although he liked Pieter von Schellenberg and could sympathise with him, he would have considered him a weaker man to have been caught in a trap by such a bullying upstart as Kreiser, whose only endearing characteristic was over-riding ambition.

So perhaps Wilhelm Hoffmeister is the hero; although I've a sneaking regard for Jagmann, who would have been alive to this day if he hadn't stopped firing when he heard the one word, Michelle, on a moonless night in March, 1945.